THE LAST STAGE FROM CEDAR STATION

The Last Stage From Cedar Station

COL. R.C. HARTJEN

The Last Stage From Cedar Station
© 2026 Ray Hartjen, Jr.

Published in Mission Viejo, California by Two Red Chairs Publishing.
ISBN 979-8-9997831-6-5 paperback
ISBN 979-8-9997831-7-2 e-book

Front & Back Cover Photography by:
Pedro_Turrini (iStock)
Cover Design by:
Ray Hartjen, Jr.
Helen Hartjen
Ray Hartjen III
Interior Design by:
Ray Hartjen III

For my wife Helen and my son Ray, without whom this book would never have been published.

Contents

Chapter 1

Sheriff Matt Horton stepped out onto the porch of the cafe, pulled his hat down to shield his eyes from the mid-morning sun, and used a toothpick to dislodge the remnants of a late breakfast of steak and eggs from between his two front teeth. That task accomplished, he leaned against the porch rail and surveyed the main street of Benton.

He couldn't help but be impressed with just how much the little Texas town had grown over the past six years. When he and his brothers had returned from the War for Southern Independence, the town had been just a shell. His brother Seth had destroyed a good bit of what was left as he had fought to rid the place of a renegade union officer named Delacourte and the other carpetbaggers who had taken over. That had been one hell of a fight, the sheriff mused, one that folks were still talking about.

As a matter of habit, Horton looked over the town, but today he searched for signs of something wrong. He had a feeling in his gut that hadn't come from Marta's cafe cooking. Something wasn't quite right, he thought, but he couldn't put his finger on it. Uneasy,

Horton started walking slowly up the street toward the barber shop and his morning shave. It was hot, but the wind was brisk and blew dust devils down the middle of the street, much to the disgust of the few people going about their business.

As Horton walked along, he suddenly saw movement across the street in the alley next to the bank. Several horses were being held there by a man he recognized immediately as Tommy Duncan, the brother of Claire, the young woman Horton was courting.

Just as Horton started over to see what was going on, four men, all with bulging saddlebags slung over their shoulders and pistols in their hands, burst through the front doors of the bank and headed for the alley and the horses.

Horton dropped to one knee as he drew his Colt.

"Halt!" he barked as he thumbed back the hammer of his pistol. "Stand where you are!"

Pandemonium broke out. The men whirled and started firing at Horton, who immediately returned the fire, killing the outlaw closest to the horses. Josh Swenson, a teller from the bank, stepped through the door of that establishment and shot another outlaw in the back at close range with a shotgun. The man was nearly cut in two.

Josh and his victory were both short-lived, however, because a third outlaw shot two holes that could have been covered with a silver dollar straight through the teller's heart. The hapless man was dead before he hit the boardwalk and rolled into the street.

The fourth outlaw snapped off a shot that cut a shallow furrow in Horton's right calf, then turned and jumped for one of the horses that young Duncan was trying with little success to control. Just as the outlaw swung himself into the saddle, the sheriff shot him in the chest, knocking him off his horse and back into the street.

As Horton swung his sights back to the outlaw who had killed the teller, Duncan let go of the other horses, slid to the side of his own mount, and made a break for it down the main street. A loose horse lunged into Horton's line of fire and caught the slug the lawman had meant for the teller's murderer. The horse fell kicking and screaming in the street. With his horse gone, the outlaw thought about his chances for survival and threw down his pistol as he yelled for quarter.

Horton swung back to take a shot at Duncan, but he couldn't get a clear shot at him or his horse. In seconds the fleeing outlaw cut into an alley and was gone from view.

From start to finish, the battle in front of the bank had lasted less than a minute. Horton stood up and dusted himself off before the startled townspeople had time to react. As the townsmen started to crowd around, the lawman limped over to the remaining outlaw and pushed him up against the wall of the bank and checked him for other weapons.

"Not so rough!" the outlaw exclaimed as the sheriff finished the search and twisted the man's arms behind him,

"Better get used to it, mister," Horton said as he snapped the handcuffs over the badman's wrists. "That hemp rope you'll be meetin' ain't gonna be none too gentle, either." Horton swung the man around and shoved him in the direction of the jail.

"Best move along smartly, or the townsfolk are likely to make that introduction sooner'n the judge will," the sheriff said softly. The outlaw looked at him with contempt, but he did start walking briskly towards the jail.

As they walked along, Horton saw his deputy, Carl Butcher, running up the street towards the bank. The sheriff stopped him and said, "Butch, go up there to the bank an' get those bodies out of sight. Find the mayor an' send him over to the jail."

Horton winced as the wound along his calf sent him another signal. "Better send the doc along, too," he added after a moment of thought. "I may have a long ride ahead of me. When you're done with that, get my horse saddled and brought around." Horton added a "please" almost as an afterthought.

Butcher knew his boss too well to waste any time asking questions, dumb or otherwise. He settled for touching the brim of his hat in a half-salute and took off running for the bank. Horton and his prisoner walked the rest of the way to the jail in silence. The street was becoming crowded as the curious made their way to the bank. Horton was glad now that the teller had been such an unlikeable cuss. If he had been better liked, there would have been real danger of a lynching that day. These Texans believed in quick and final justice.

Rufus Pflugg, the mayor, was the first to show up at the jail. He was a large man who lately had been developing a modest pot belly, and he aspired to be governor of Texas. Based on others who had held that office, Horton thought that if Pflugg ever became a little more inept or senile, he might just stand a chance of being elected.

"What's going on, Matt?" the mayor inquired. "What was that commotion up by the bank?"

Horton quickly told him what had happened. After a moment or two of silence, the mayor spoke.

"I know you're goin' after the Duncan kid. You couldn't show your face around here if you didn't," he said.

"Tell me something' I don't already know, Rufus," the sheriff responded. "I'll bring him in 'cause it's my job an' because a man got hisself killed for tryin' to be a hero. But I ain't takin' no posse with me."

"Why not?" Pflugg asked.

"'Cause Duncan's just probably the best horseman around, an' I know he's well-mounted. I got a good horse, too, an' a posse ain't no faster than the speed of the slowest horse. I ain't lookin' to make this chase my life's work," Horton answered.

"Makes sense to me," the mayor said after a long pause, "but if you had more folks along, no one could blame you if the kid gives you the slip. Then folks would know that you'd done your best."

"I'll do my best without folks watchin'," Horton spat back testily. "Anytime them folks out there ain't satisfied with the job I do, I'll be more than happy to leave office. I'm only doin' this job 'cause you an' some of the rich folks in town asked me to do your dirty work in the first place."

"Don't get your dander up, Matt," the mayor said soothingly. "I just was tryin' to make things easier for you."

"Don't try so damned hard next time," Horton suggested tersely. "You sound too much like a politician."

Mayor Pflugg drew himself up to his full height, took a deep breath, and started to say something. He thought better of it, however, and put his hat on instead as he started for the door.

"Let me know when you get back," he ordered as he shut the door behind him before the sheriff could answer. Face had been saved.

By the time the doctor arrived and bandaged the groove in his leg and Matt had gathered up his kit to start after Tommy Duncan, more than an hour had passed. Even if a posse had been practical, Horton knew that he wouldn't have taken one. This was something he had to do alone. It was a matter of honor. As he pulled himself into the saddle, he reviewed the results of the robbery attempt: three outlaws and a teller were dead, a fourth outlaw was locked up in jail, and all the money had been recovered. All there was left to do was to bring in Tommy Duncan. That was enough.

Horton thought that bringing in that kid might just possibly prove to be the toughest thing he had ever had to do.

Chapter 2

U sually Matt Horton was an even-tempered man, slow to anger and quite unlikely to be baited by some smart-talking youth eager to make a reputation for himself. In fact, he could only remember a couple of times during the five years that he'd worn a badge when anyone had been foolish enough to even try to build a reputation at his expense. One of those had died quickly and violently when he had proven to be unskilled with the Colt he carried, the other had been laughed out of town when his nerve failed him at the crucial moment.

But this day had not been a usual one. Horton was tired, dirty, foul-smelling, and evil-tempered as the result of his ride in hard pursuit of the lone survivor of that abortive bank robbery six days earlier.

It was mid-morning when he rode into the stage relay station and trading post at Cedar Station. Horton guessed that Tommy Duncan was about two hours ahead of him and opening the distance between them every hour. The sheriff figured that he had about three days in which to catch the man before they reached the Mexican border at El Paso, although he had no intention of stopping at the border if he had not caught Duncan by then. There was more to this chase than a failed attempt to rob the Benton bank. There had been the dead man on the walk in front of the bank, a man whose only crime had been to try to stop the outlaws from escaping with the bank's money. That changed the rules as far as Horton was concerned.

There was also the fact that the sole outlaw not dead or in jail was the brother of the woman Horton wanted to marry. Horton could not or would not stop until he brought the kid home, either as his prisoner or tied across his saddle. If the kid got away, no one in Benton would believe that he had not let him escape. If Horton did catch him, the town was sure to hang the kid in front of the courthouse, and it did not take a fortune teller to predict that Claire would never consent to marry Matt if that happened. Horton felt like he was caught between a rock and a hard place, where there was no way he could come out of this thing pleasing everybody. Hell, he thought, there's no way I'm gonna please anybody. This feeling accounted in part for his vile mood as he reined up in front of the station.

Horton dismounted, pushed his hat back on his head, and wiped the sweat and dust from his face with the large red bandana he produced from his hip pocket. When he finished mopping his brow, he led his horse around the corner of the building and over to the large stone corral, where he proceeded to unsaddle the big grey and turn it in with the others penned up there.

He left the saddle next to the gate. Pedro O'Brien, the owner of Cedar Station, always kept a few head of good horses around to trade to passing folks who were in a hurry to get to the edge of nowhere. In fact, most of the remounts had been purchased from the Circle H, the ranch that Horton and his three brothers owned and which his brother Marcus operated.

As he turned his horse loose, Horton recognized the animal that Duncan had been riding. It was standing straddle-legged in the middle of the corral, head down and worn out. The sheriff walked over and patted the big animal. The sweat was mostly dried, he saw, and the animal wasn't blowing, either. Horton wasn't happy. It was clear to him that the kid had been pushing his mount to the limit of its endurance and had probably widened the gap between the two men. It was also more than likely that the kid had traded for the best remount that O'Brien had on the place. Seven years of living with the Comanche had turned the kid into a keen judge of horseflesh. The irony of the fact that the kid was probably escaping on a Horton horse was not lost on the sheriff.

Horton swatted at a large horsefly that seemed intent on making a meal of the lawman's ear and shuffled through the dust to the back of the station. He glanced at the three horses tied at the hitching rail, but he did not recognize the brands. The horses were nothing to brag on, he decided, but the saddle on the best of the three caught his eye. It was a fancy, hand-tooled rig with a lot of silver stuck all over it.

In a land where the Comanche and now even some Apache were not willing to concede that the white man ruled, it was unusual to see fancy trappings that reflected the light and drew the attention of anyone within five miles. Rigs like that could prove to be down-right unhealthy for the owner. Horton decided that it probably belonged to some fancy-pants out of El Paso who didn't have to work for a living. That made him mad, too. Everyone ought to work, he thought, as his temper got worse by the minute. He stomped the rest of the way to the back door and let himself in.

Horton closed the door behind him softly and stood there in the cool gloom of the large adobe building un-til his eyes adjusted to the change of light. He did not need to look at the room to know where everything was. He had been there many times before and knew every inch of the single room. Trade goods and food stuff lined the shelves along the walls on either side of him. Hardware items, ammunition, a gun rack, and a pistol case dominated the opposite wall. To his right, a bar extended along the end of the room, and a cooking fireplace and several tables were at the opposite end of the room. He turned his head to look at the bar and found Pedro perched upon his favorite stool, polishing his glasses and trying to ignore the boisterous talk of the three young men drinking at the far end of the bar.

Horton looked at the men carefully. They were all young, barely out of their teens. The one in the middle was a little taller than the other two. He was dressed in black and had silver coins fixed to his hat band. Horton guessed that he belonged to the fancy-rigged horse tied up outside. The other two men bore a strong resemblance to one another and were obviously competing for the attention of the man in black. Each of the men wore a pair of heavy Colt Model 1860 Army pistols tied low, butts forward and rigged for cross-draw.

The sheriff didn't know the men, but he knew the type. The tied-down, cross-draw rigs marked them as tinhorns who fancied themselves to be bad men with a gun. In any sort of fight, they probably would spray a lot of lead before they got close to the target. In the years since the end of the War Between the States, the fast draw had started to get a lot of attention, largely undeserved, in Horton's opinion. He still believed that it was not the first shot fired that counted, but rather the first shot that hit the target that made the difference.

He wore his own pistol, a brand-new Model 1872 Open Top Colt .44, high up on his right hip where it was out of his way when he was working, but still handy enough if he needed it in a hurry. He also had a five-shot Model 1862 Colt Police Special tucked into his belt at the small of his back for emergencies. He'd learned the value of a hold-out gun from his brother Seth. In town he usually carried a sawed-off shotgun when he made his rounds. It took a foolish or a very drunk man to argue with those twin ten-gage muzzles.

On this chase, however, Horton carried in a saddle scabbard the Model 1860 Henry that his brother Seth had given him right after the war. Both the Henry and the Model 1872 Colt he carried were chambered for the same .44 caliber rimfire cartridge, which was quite an advantage when space for carrying extra ammunition was limited.

Horton walked slowly toward the end of the bar furthest from the noisy trio and signaled Pedro for a beer. The jovial bartender slid off his stool, drew a large glass of the amber fluid from a keg beneath the bar, and slid it down to Matt. He followed along behind the beer slowly until he stood across from Horton.

"Whatcha doin' way down here, my friend?" O'Brien asked, a broad grin splitting his swarthy features. "You get lost again, or somethin'?"

Horton took a swallow of his beer and was surprised to find that it was almost cold. He swallowed again eagerly, then set his glass on the bar and wiped his mouth on his sleeve.

"Or somethin', I reckon, you old horse thief," Horton said as he shook the large paw Pedro had extended over the bar. "Fellow tried to make a little withdrawal at our bank the other day an' the town folk took offense. Matter of fact, he was ridin' that chestnut that's damn near dead out there in your corral. From the looks of him, I hope you didn't give the boy anything much in trade."

Pedro drew back a little and cursed softly under his breath. "I'll be damned," he said. "I never would a thought it. He didn't look old enough to be weaned, let alone be off robbin' banks."

Matt took another pull at his beer, then said, "He's just nineteen. Name's Tommy Duncan, an' he's a damn tough young man. The Comanche raided his folks' place about a ten years back. The rest of the family forted up in the house an' held 'em off 'til help came. Tommy was comin' back from a neighbor's place an' got caught. He spent the next seven years livin' with them Indians an' learnin' how to be a warrior. There ain't a better horseman in the country, an' he's pretty damn good with a bow, knife, or any kind of firearm. He left Benton a year ago 'cause he was feelin' pretty restless an' cooped up. He showed up again six days ago with that bunch who thought to get rich at the expense of the bank's depositors."

"You sure know a lot about the kid," Pedro observed.

"I ought to. I was fixin' to marry his sister 'til this business came up," the sheriff lamented.

A tall, slender man entered the room, walked to the bar, and waited patiently for the bartender to finish his conversation. Pedro moved down the bar in the man's direction. The cowboy ordered a beer and drank it down without taking it from his mouth. When he finished, he set the glass carefully on the bar, wiped his mustache on his sleeve, and flipped a dime onto the bar.

Pedro scooped up the coin and put it in the till.

"Thanks, Stubby. See you the next time you pass through," the bartender said to the man as he headed for the door.

The man waved in reply and closed the door softly behind him.

Pedro went back to the sheriff.

"Why'd you call that man 'Stubby'?" Horton asked. "He's gotta be two, three inches over six foot, at least."

"Ah, my friend, it's a sad story. When Stubby was a lot younger, he romanced about every female between fifteen and fifty that he could find. He wasn't particular whether they was married or not. All they had to be was willin'. An' since he was a good lookin' man an' they was generally lonely, most was willin'.

"Anyway, one day Stubby was caught in a 'compromisin' position', as they say, when a rancher came home a whole lot earlier than his wife thought he would. Well, Stubby had enough time to jump into his pants, stomp on his boots, and make a break for it through the bedroom window. He made it to his horse an' took off like there wasn't gonna be no tomorrow, which there wouldn't of been if that rancher had caught him.

"The rancher, now he wasn't quite done with Stubby yet. He went into the front room, got his .50 caliber Sharps down from off of the mantel piece, slapped a cartridge into the breech an' walked to the front porch. Stubby was damn near out of sight by then, ridin' as hard as he could. The rancher drew down on Stubby an' fired. The bullet went about half a mile, went plum through the cantle, and blew off one of his cajones an' all but about an inch of the thing that he was proudest of. Fortunately, the bullet lodged in the pommel an' didn't go on to kill the horse, too. Stubby tied a piggin' string around the stump an' made it to a doctor before he bled to death. Ever since then folks have called him 'Stubby' an' husbands an' fathers have been breathin' a whole lot easier."

"That's a hell of a story," Horton said as he choked with laughter. "Sorta painfully funny, you might say."

Further conversation was interrupted by the trio at the other end of the bar.

"Hey, old man!" the leader of the group exclaimed. "Quit botherin' Mex. He's got customers down here, too."

Matthew turned toward the speaker. "What's your problem, sonny?" he said softly as Pedro scurried away to provide another bottle to the trio.

"You're my problem, old man," the man in black sneered as he started moving toward Horton. "You're standing there yappin' with this fool while we're dyin' of thirst. Maybe you ought to leave so you don't distract the greaser again."

Horton stood away from the bar as the speaker stopped about five feet away, thumbs hooked in his gun belt. Horton's badge was hidden under his vest, but he suspected that the kid had downed enough booze so that the badge wouldn't have made any difference, anyway.

"I don't much care for your tone of voice or your choice of words, boy," Horton responded. "You owe Mister O'Brien here an apology."

The man in black smiled, revealing uneven, half-rotten teeth. "Old man, all I owe either of you is a belly full of lead," he said as he unhooked his thumbs from his gun belt and crossed his arms in preparation for a draw. "You can either draw your piece or leave," he smirked.

The man's two companions moved away from the bar and stood next to the gunman. "Yeah," said the shorter of the other two men. "Why don't cha draw old man? Jack ain't killed nothin' since breakfast." The pair giggled at their little joke.

Pedro chose that moment to speak up.

"Please, gentlemen, let's not have any trouble in here. There's whiskey enough for everybody."

The man called Jack turned away from the sheriff and backhanded Pedro across the face. "Shut up, greaser. This don't concern you," he said sharply.

It was then that Horton hit the man.

While the attention of the trio was momentarily focused on the bartender, Horton made his move. He stepped forward, grabbed a handful of the gunman's shirt and swung a powerful right that came straight from the shoulder. The blow had all of the sheriff's two hundred pounds behind it and connected squarely with the young tough's nose. Horton smiled coldly as he heard bone break and saw blood squirt. He jerked the gunman toward him as he cocked his right and hit him again, this time connecting solidly with the point of the loudmouth's chin. The man's eyes rolled back in his head as his knees collapsed.

Horton threw the unconscious gunman at the other two men, who were trying to drag their pistols out of their holsters. The trio fell into a tangled pile at the end of the bar. As the two toughs who were still conscious tried to untangle themselves from their leader, Horton drew his pistol and stepped forward. As the first man got free and started to rise, Matt struck him along the temple with the barrel. The man collapsed without a sound. Horton wondered almost idly if he'd killed the man and was a little surprised to find that he really didn't care. He turned his attention to the third man, who almost had made it to his feet. Horton jammed his pistol into the terrified man's face. He misjudged the distance between himself and the other man just a little. The muzzle hit the man's front teeth, snapping them off at the gum. The man started to scream, then thought better of it. He just stood there, shaking all over.

Horton stepped back a little and lowered the pistol in his fist.

"Boy, I want you to ease them hog legs out of your belt between your thumb an' your forefinger, one at a time. Use your left hand and be real slow about it, too. You got my dander up, an' I got a mind to use this Colt if you give me just a little cause," Horton said coldly.

The man did as he was told.

"Now do the same to your two pals," Matt instructed. "Pedro, I'd take it as a personal favor if you went out back an' collected these boys' saddle guns. They look to be the back-shootin' type to me."

Pedro nodded as he wiped a trickle of blood from the corner of his mouth. He paused as he looked at Jack's unconscious form on the floor, then stomped on his outstretched hand. Several bones snapped like dry twigs. Jack didn't even groan.

"Maybe he won't be so damn quick to slap a man the next time," the station owner muttered as he made his way out the back door.

The last gunman completed his chore and stood up. "We didn't mean nothin', mister," he whined after he spat out the two broken teeth. "Please don't do nothin' more." He winced as he sucked some air over the broken stumps of his teeth.

"You 'didn't mean nothin','" Horton mimicked. "What you meant to do was kill me 'cause you had nothin' better to do. The only reason I don't shoot you where you stand is 'cause I'm wearin' this here badge," he said as he flipped back his vest to reveal the star.

Horton paused for a moment as if to make up his mind, then he continued.

"You take them friends of yours out back an' tie 'em on their horses. Then you get on yours an' head east just as fast as you can go. I'm tellin' you now, an' you tell them punks when they wake up, that none of you've got what it takes to be a good gunman. If you want to live, you need to change your line of work, but whatever you decide, I want you to do it outside of Texas. If I ever run across any of you again, I'll shoot you on sight." He looked directly into the terrified youth's eyes. "That's a promise that I'd like for you to believe, boy," he said, almost in a whisper.

The young gunman bobbed his head up and down in acknowledgement of the message. It was quite plain from the spreading stain in the crotch of his pants that he believed Horton. Suddenly the old days of farming in Mississippi looked very good to him. He vowed to himself that he would not stop until he made it back home, and he thought that his brother would feel the same way, too, when he woke up. Jack could rot in hell for all he cared.

Horton watched as the youth dragged his companions outside and loaded them onto their horses. Pedro had to help the man a little, but finally the job was finished, and the man rode off leading the horses laden with the unconscious cargo. Pedro walked over to Horton and put his hand on the sheriff's shoulder.

"Thank you, my friend, for speaking up for me. You didn't need to go to the trouble, though. I've been called worse things by far better men."

Horton nodded his head and said, "Well, I guess I have, too, amigo. It's always the little men who try to make themselves bigger by puttin' someone else down. They are stupid, shallow people who can't be counted on for nothin' but treachery." A twinkle came into Horton's eye. "But if it will make you feel any better, my friend, what I really took offense to was bein' called 'old man.' Hell, I ain't even thirty yet!"

"Then you ought not to be so quick to get mad," Pedro advised. "You're so dirty an' ugly, you look like you're sixty."

The two men laughed together for a while, then went back inside. Horton finished his beer and drank a second as Pedro heated up some stew and set a place at one of the tables. Horton cleaned the plate quickly and sopped up the gravy with a thick slice of bread.

"I guess Tommy Duncan took the best horse in the corral," Matt said as he licked the last traces of gravy from his moustache. "How do you want to trade for the best of what you got left?"

Pedro smiled his most disarming smile. "Would I cheat a friend? Wait—don't answer that. You don't want nothin' I got left in the corral, at least not after you see what I got in the stable." He paused for a moment as if to tantalize the sheriff a little, then he said, "I got a big, four-year-old roan out there that I got from your brother last year. He's a Standardbred-Thoroughbred mix with a little Morgan thrown in for spice. He's sixteen hands at the shoulder an' got more bottom than any horse I ever owned. You can't trade for him, but I'll loan him to you 'til you come back. I seen your grey while I was out pickin' up those rifles. He should be ready for you to ride before you get by here again."

Horton remembered the roan. If there ever was an animal made for a long pursuit, that horse was it. Matt went outside with Pedro and looked the horse over. He was just as Horton remembered, hard-muscled and ready for a long ride. While the station owner saddled the animal, Horton walked over by the stable and made good use of the privy. He knew that it might be a long time before he got the chance to experience the luxury of another.

As Horton prepared to mount, Pedro handed him one of the rifles that he had taken from the gunmen's scabbards.

"Matt, maybe you might want to take this along," O'Brien suggested. "This 1866 Winchester rifle is lighter than your Henry, easier to load, an' won't jam up nearly as quick. It shoots the same cartridge, too. Better than that, it's free."

The lawman took the rifle and worked the action. A fresh cartridge flipped out from the top of the receiver. Matt reloaded the weapon, took his Henry from the saddle scabbard, and slipped the Winchester into its place. He handed the Henry to Pedro.

"Hold on to this for me, friend. It's my brother's. I'll get it when I come back for my horse. If you get rid of either one, you'd better be prepared to fight."

The two men grinned at each other and then shook hands. Horton mounted the roan and set off in the noon heat after Tommy Duncan. He had already forgotten about the brief fight at the station. The only thing that the sheriff could think about was the fact that he'd probably just lost another hour to the fugitive. He was three hours behind his quarry and not closing the gap.

Chapter 3

The lead that Tommy Duncan had been building over the past six days started to diminish about three hours after he left Cedar Station. Duncan had spent little time at the station, pausing only long enough to strike a trade for the chestnut gelding he now rode. He had thought of buying a few more supplies but decided that he didn't need to carry the extra weight or lose the added time. He had ridden from the station like a Comanche, putting as much distance behind him as he could for the first half-hour. After that he slowed his pace and started to take some pains to cover his trail.

He took the trouble to cover his trail because he knew Matt Horton. He liked and feared the lawman. Not for the first time he kicked himself mentally for being stupid enough to try robbing the bank in Horton's town.

Horton had been a hero to the boy before his capture by the Comanche, and after he had made his escape, the lawman had gone out of his way to help the boy fit back into the community. They had hunted together many times, and Duncan knew that Horton could track and shoot with the best of them. He knew that it would take every trick in the book, as well as a lot of luck, to throw the lawman off his trail.

Duncan crested a small hill and reined the horse into a small grove of cedar. He took a pair of binoculars from his saddlebag and studied his backtrail as his horse snorted and swatted flies with his tail. It was well past noon, and the heat was creating waves that made it difficult to study the terrain.

The fugitive was finally satisfied that his pursuer was far behind. He returned the binoculars to his saddlebag and dismounted.

He knew this land as well as he knew his own hand. He had traveled through it many times while he was a captive, and later, when they thought that he was one of them, he had hunted there for his adopted family.

He had killed his first man not more than a mile from where he now sat. He had been twelve at the time, and the man had been a Comanchero who was determined to take the boy's horse. Tommy had fired an arrow into the man's back as he had tried to ride off.

Duncan forced the memory from his mind and concentrated on the task at hand. He removed some rawhide from his bedroll and cut it into squares which he tied with thongs to his horse's hooves. The ground ahead of him was starting to become rocky. The rawhide would keep the horse's shoes from marking the rock and would make the hoofprints on sand and dirt less distinct. Duncan had no hope that this trick would throw Horton off his trail for very long, but then again, he might get lucky. Besides, he had another trick up his sleeve.

The youth had been following a direct route from Benton to El Paso for six days. He knew that Matt Horton would not let a little thing like an international border stop his pursuit, so Duncan planned to ride on towards El Paso for one more day, then cut due south to the Rio Grande. From there he would follow the river southeast and cross into Mexico at Eagle Pass. The plan required only two things to succeed: Horton had to believe that he was headed for El Paso, and Duncan had to make the lawman lose his trail by tomorrow morning.

Duncan finished tying the last thong and remounted his horse. The animal didn't much like his new footwear and showed his feelings by snorting and prancing around. Duncan talked softly to the animal in the way he had learned from his Comanche brothers. The horse quickly calmed and the youth reined him out of the cedars and on towards El Paso.

The kid moved carefully to avoid breaking branches and leaving other signs of his passage. He kept his horse off the skyline as best he could without altering his course.

Five hundred yards away, a set of black, hate-filled eyes watched the kid put rawhide pads on his horse's hooves. Yellow Horse had seen faint movement below him. Hoping for a quick end to his hunt, he had moved closer and closer until he found the source of the movement.

Yellow Horse was a little disappointed when he discovered that what he had seen was not a deer but a man. He rode on the hunt; he had not set his mind for war. He started to turn away, to move silently back to his horse and continue his hunt, when something compelled him to look again at the man in front of him. There was something familiar about that man ....

The Indian gave a start, barely noticeable to anyone had they been watching, but Yellow Horse felt as though a buffalo had fallen on him. He knew that man! Silently the Indian crept closer as his mind was filled with the memory of what had gone before.

Yellow Horse could not believe his luck. The spirits of his ancestors must be shining on him this day, for the man he had just seen was certainly the white-eyed youth that his father had captured on a raiding party many years ago. Swift Eagle he had been named, and he had lived with Yellow Horse, his older brother, and his parents for seven winters. They had lived together as brothers, as close as two people could be, until the time of the Great Treachery. In the aftermath to that event, Spotted Calf, his father, had lost two sons: one of his own blood who had died with a knife in his back, and the other the white-eye who had called himself son to Yellow Horse's father. The white-eye had just vanished, his leaving an open admission to the whole tribe of his guilt.

Yellow Horse tried to stop the images that were flooding his memory and clouding his vision like a heavy mist, but he could not. He remembered the sadness in his lodge, his mother's tears, and the pain in his father's eyes, and he remembered also that his father had never quite gotten over the death of his older son, who had always clearly been his favorite. Yellow Horse had hoped that after his brother's death he might find favor in his father's eyes, but that had not happened. Somehow anything Yellow Horse did fell short of Spotted Calf's expectation.

Yellow Horse watched Duncan mount his horse and head towards the spot where the sun left the sky. Hatred burned deep within him, and he thought to mount his own horse and give chase to this white man who had caused so much pain in his family.

But something seemed to hold him back. Swift Eagle had been a skillful hunter, a strong fighter, and a dangerous enemy. In truth, Yellow Horse had always been envious of him, and perhaps just a little afraid. That thought caused him to pause now.

"My father and all our people should see this man's death," he reasoned. "Perhaps then I will find favor in the eyes of my father."

Yellow Horse ran back to his horse, mounted, and headed back to the place where his people camped. They would all share in the death of Swift Eagle, and he would become great in the eyes of his father for having discovered him.

Tommy Duncan was remembering, too. He knew this country well. He had hunted there with Spotted Calf, Yellow Horse, and Running Buffalo, Spotted Calf's older son. It had been Running Buffalo who had always kept an eye on him, never giving him a chance to slip away. For seven long years Duncan had never been left alone for very long, in spite of the fact that Spotted Calf had called him his son.

But there were good times, too. The feasts after the hunts, the learning to hunt, to track and stalk the game that seemed to abound everywhere. And there were the evenings when he got older when he discovered passion in the thickets near the river. Yes, there had been good times, but always there was in him the desire to go home to his family.

Then one day, for no reason that he could see, Running Buffalo was nowhere to be found. Duncan had ridden away from the camp as hard as he could. He had used every trick he knew to hide his tracks, and he had succeeded in losing his followers. It had taken him nearly a month, but he had found his way home, only to find his parents dead and the people he had once called friends suspicious of him. He had moved in with his sister in town, but somehow the town had seemed too small, too confining, and he chafed under the stares of the townsmen and the comments they made about him being a "white Injun," as if he were deaf.

Except for Matt Horton. The sheriff had gone out of his way to be kind. They had hunted together, talked at length, and had developed a strong friendship. Matt had understood when he had told him that he was going to ride out, to start a life of his own somewhere else, somewhere where people didn't know him.

Then last month he had suddenly done something that was really stupid. The thirty dollars a month he was making riding for an outfit north of Waco didn't seem to come to much. He and four of his new friends decided to quit the job and try the outlaw trail. Benton had been their first job, and he cursed himself for being ten kinds of a fool for ever leaving the ranch, dull as the job was. Now he was broke, running for his life, and perhaps worst of all, he had Matt Horton on his trail.

Duncan crested a small rise and made his way down the other side to a long, flat-looking plain. Looks were deceptive, though. Erosion had cut great chunks from the earth, creating sudden drops that were all but hidden by the thick growth of cedar and mesquite until a rider was almost upon them, forcing the unknowing to detour up to a mile to get around them. An army could be hidden in those draws and arroyos, and ambush sites abounded.

But Duncan knew where he was going. He rode with purpose, threading his way around obstacles and stopping from time to time to replace the rawhide pads on his horse's hooves. Familiar landmarks guided him, and not for the first time he mentally thanked Running Buffalo for being such a good teacher.

The terrain suddenly gave way to deep chasms and treacherous shale. Duncan slowed his speed and skillfully guided his mount along the rim of a steep canyon. He knew of an old game trail, seldom used, that would take him quickly to the canyon floor and to water. The afternoon shadows were growing long, and Duncan planned to spend the night at or very near the spring.

And then the unthinkable happened. Duncan's horse was sure-footed enough, but the shale over which they were riding suddenly gave way and the horse stumbled, then scrambled to regain its footing. He very nearly succeeded, but then more shale gave way and the horse and rider tumbled toward the bottom of the canyon.

The kid somehow flung himself from the saddle and managed to hang on to the reins. He dug his heels in as best he could and tried to stop the downward plunge of his horse. Miraculously both Tommy and the horse stopped sliding about a hundred yards from the trail. As both regained their feet, Tommy walked over to check out his horse.

There were cuts and scrapes on the horse, of course, and a patch of hide about the size of the palm of a man's hand was hanging from the animal's left hip. The horse was shaking all over, and its nostrils were full-blown. But the real damage had been done to the right forefoot. Either in the mad scramble for footing or in the fall, the pad and shoe had been torn from the hoof, and the hoof itself had been split up into the frog.

The horse was lame and would be lame for some time. Duncan was now afoot. In spite of the heat, he felt a cold chill touch his spine, and for the first time since his capture by the Comanche he knew real fear. His chances had been bad enough with a good mount beneath him. Now everything was changed. He wondered if his luck had run out, and he shivered again. He knew that Horton was coming.

Chapter 4

Yellow Horse rode hard toward the Comanche camp. He cared nothing for his mount, which was laboring hard in the full heat of the afternoon. Whenever the animal slowed, the determined rider lashed him into greater effort. Yellow Horse paid no attention to the branches of mesquite and cedar that tore at his body and his leggings. He thought only of his purpose and his hate for Swift Eagle.

By the time Yellow Horse reached the camp, his mount was stumbling from fatigue and was bleeding freely from cuts inflicted by the brush through which they had ridden. He was also bleeding heavily from the nose, a sure sign that from this day the animal would be fit only for use by the camp children. If game became scarce, it would be the first animal to be shared among the camp's cook pots. Dogs started barking as the warrior rode through the camp in search of his father.

Yellow Horse leaped to the ground in front of Spotted Calf's tepee and hurried inside. Curious people from other tepees came out to see what all the excitement was about. Yellow Horse ignored them.

"My father," he said as he dropped to the ground beside Spotted Calf, "I have some great news for you."

Spotted Calf looked up slowly from the rifle that he had been cleaning.

"I heard you ride through the camp like one possessed by evil spirits, and I can hear your horse blowing from here. What could be so important that you would kill your horse to tell of it?"

"Father, I have found Swift Eagle," Yellow Horse said, his black eyes glinting hatefully. "I myself have been close enough to him to count the hairs on his head."

"And you did not kill him?" the old man thundered as he leaped to his feet. "You saw the killer of your own brother, and you did not cut out his heart?" He looked accusingly at Yellow Horse and said scornfully, "Have I fathered a coward?"

Yellow Horse felt heat rising to his face and at that moment he knew the hate he felt for the father who had always scorned him. But Yellow Horse feared Spotted Calf, too, and he fought to keep his tone respectful and humble.

"I am not afraid of Swift Eagle," he said truthfully, "but I knew that my father would want to avenge the blood of Running Buffalo. I came to lead you to the killer of my brother, that we might both share in his death."

Spotted Calf looked at Yellow Horse for a moment or two, as if he were trying to look into his younger son's soul. He made a decision and spoke more calmly.

"It is well that you have spoken as you have. Swift Eagle has shamed his family and your brother's spirit cries out for revenge. You are now my eldest son. It is you that the honor of capturing this devil should go. Ride swiftly and find this man again. And when you find him, bring him back to me. He shall die a slow death at the hands of the women of the camp. It will be a fitting end for a coward who would put a knife into the back of his adopted brother."

Yellow Horse got to his feet swiftly and left the te-pee without a word, a look of satisfaction on his face. It took him only a few minutes to prepare a fresh horse and to paint it and himself for war. He sang an ancient war chant of his people as he rode from the camp in search of Swift Eagle.

"They will sing of this day around the fires of my grandchildren," he said to his horse as he rode back towards the white man that he hated so much, the man who was his blood brother.

Tommy Duncan cursed under his breath. He cursed the heat, he cursed the bad luck that had crippled his horse, and he cursed his stupidity that had led him to be pursued by the only man he truly respected and would want to call his friend.

After inspecting his horse, the young outlaw knew that he could not be ridden another step. Duncan cut off the other pads that covered the horse's hooves, removed the saddle and bridle, and turned the horse loose. The animal limped off a few steps, then looked back at him and nickered softly.

"Get along with you now," Duncan said as he waved his hat at the animal. "The least you can do is lay a false trail for me."

As if the animal knew what the outlaw had said and had decided to help, the horse took off down the trail at an awkward trot.

Duncan knew that the horse would not be able to go far and that Horton would know immediately that he was afoot as soon as he saw the site where they had fallen. But some miracle might still happen, he told himself. In his heart he heard a small voice say, "Not a chance!" He believed that voice.

Duncan found a spot under a mesquite tree where he could hide his saddle and still have a reasonable chance of finding it again. He took with him only his Henry rifle, the one canteen that had not broken when the horse fell, and the small amount of food that he could stuff into his shirt. He left behind his boots, too, replacing them with moccasins from his bedroll. After some thought he took a ground sheet, a blanket, and his lariat, too. He decided that he could always discard them if they became too heavy. He wished that he had a change of clothes, for the fall had torn his shirt and pants in several places.

"If I'd have had enough money for new clothes, I wouldn't have tried to hold up that damned bank in the first place," he said to himself as he set out towards the water he hoped that he could still find. He decided that he still needed to make Horton think that he was headed toward El Paso, so he left a few signs as he moved easily through the brush. His plan was to find the water, spend the night, and then head for Eagle Pass at dawn. As he walked, he prayed that something would happen to slow Horton enough that his plan would work. But he had small hope that Horton could be fooled for long. Besides, he told himself, God is unlikely to answer the prayers of a thief. He knew that his chances of making good his escape were somewhere between slim and none, but he knew that he must still try. The only other alternative was a long fall with a short rope, and he desperately wanted to avoid that.

Duncan thought of trying to strike a bargain with God. "If you help me escape, Lord, I'll become a preacher." He laughed ruefully when he heard himself say the words. If he didn't believe what he said, God wouldn't, either.

"I dealt the hand; I guess I'm gonna have to play the cards myself," he said softly. "I can't make any more mistakes if I want to get out of this alive."

Duncan quickened his pace. It was a long way to that water.

Chapter 5

Horton could see that Tommy Duncan had left Cedar Station as fast as the fresh horse could take him. He could also see that the boy had not changed his direction. His trail pointed like an arrow towards El Paso.

Little bells went off somewhere in Horton's head.

"It's too easy," he said to the roan. "That kid's one of the best horsemen in the state, an' he knows every trick the Comanche ever knew, an' maybe some that they don't. A man'd be a fool to think that this boy wouldn't try to cover his trail if he wasn't up to somethin'. We'd better watch careful."

The roan snorted as if in reply, and Horton laughed. Nevertheless, he kept his pace slow and steady. He had no intention of walking into an ambush, and he knew that the kid was smart enough and good enough to pull one off if he wasn't careful. During the war he had learned at some cost not to underestimate Yankees, and he was damned if he was going to underestimate this boy Duncan now, either.

The ground was deceptive. It appeared to be gently rolling, with mesquite and cedar covering nearly all of it. But hidden by this growth were deep arroyos and gullies where the ground had been washed away by rains that had fallen before the time of Cortez. And death lurked in these arroyos.

For the unwary there was death in the hot, dry, and forbidding land itself. If a man knew where the water was and paced himself so that he didn't kill his mount or wasn't set afoot, he had an even chance for survival. But if a man could not find water or was set afoot, or was just plain unlucky, then his chances for survival were slim.

Then there were the animals that roamed freely. Javelina, the wild boar that smelled like skunk and had huge tusks, dwelled in the land, ready to rip the unwary man or horse to ribbons. These beasts could be as heavy as a man and twice as mean, with skins thick enough to turn aside all but the perfectly placed bullet.

There were cats, too, in various kinds, who avoided man when they could, and who fought viciously when they couldn't. And there were snakes, rattlers who soaked up the sun on rocky ledges and hid under low branches in the mesquite, ready to strike and leave a man to die a slow, painful death. But the most dangerous animals in the brush were those on two legs.

During the war, while the Union Army was fully engaged in the east and nearly every Texan between the ages of fifteen and fifty had gone east, too, to fight with Hood or in one of the other Texas brigades, the Comanche had come back to reclaim lost hunting grounds. The Apache, too, had moved east and north, to raid and to kill anyone who was Anglo or Mexican, or, for that matter, who was not Apache. Most of the Anglo and Mexican ranchers had either been killed in these raids or driven into the larger towns and cities for protection. It was only now, more than six years after the humiliation at Appomattox courthouse, that the US Cavalry and the returned veterans had begun the drive to clear the Indians from the land that they claimed as their own. One thing was sure: the Comanche and the Apache would not leave quietly.

And the most dangerous killers of the brush were the Comancheros, Indian and Mexican bandits who robbed, raped, and plundered everything that they could find on either side of the border. They owed allegiance to no man or tribe and were regarded as renegades by everyone, Anglo, Mexican, and Indian alike. They were also feared by anyone who was sane.

The man who traveled quickly through this land was a fool, and Horton was anything but that. He stopped frequently to check the terrain through his binoculars, and he looked continuously for signs that he was not alone as he rode. Twice during the afternoon, he crossed the tracks of unshod ponies. Hunting parties, he thought. The parties were small, from five to eight riders and no extra horses. These men were after meat, not scalps, but they could be dangerous if they were led by a hot head or were surprised by a lone rider who looked like he might be easy picking.

Each time Horton dismounted and checked the tracks. From the way the tracks were caving in on the sides and the horse droppings had nearly dried, the sheriff guessed that the tracks were four or five hours old. But with two parties out, Horton knew that there would be others out as well. There would be a village not far off and he would do well to make his camp that night a cold one. He had had no problem with the Comanche, but that happy situation was more the result of avoidance than it was the product of his reputation or anything that he had done to earn their friendship. Horton was a firm believer in the theory that if you don't tempt a cougar, then you won't get scratched.

It was late afternoon when Horton cut the sign of Yellow Horse. The lone rider troubled the lawman, and he was surprised that the warrior had ridden away so fast. The Indian village must be very close, he thought, for anyone to ride at that speed. No horse could be expected to long survive a pace like that. And gnawing at the back of his mind was the question why the lone warrior had not attacked Duncan. The sheriff thought about that as he rode one.

Horton smiled at the thought of Duncan padding the hooves of his horse. He had done it well, but only a pilgrim would have been fooled by it. The prints were less distinct, but they still were there, and there were marks wherever two stones were rubbed together. There were also horsehairs to be found from time to time in the brush, and of course there were the occasional horse droppings. From these he determined that he was not falling further behind and perhaps he was even gaining on the kid.

The long shadows of dusk were sweeping over the land when Horton came across the spot where Duncan and his horse had fallen. The story was all there for anyone who could read signs. The lawman saw the broken shale, the horseshoe, the footpads, and the dried blood. Within minutes he found the horse and not long after he found the cache where Duncan had hidden his saddle and boots.

Horton stepped down from his horse and sat down on a rock to think. Absentmindedly he fumbled in his vest pocket for the makings of a smoke. He cursed silently to himself when he found himself doing it. Claire had complained long and bitterly about his smoking, calling it a filthy habit and likening kissing him to kissing a spittoon. When faced with a choice between smoking and the delights that Claire had to offer, he had given up smoking. It was at times like this, however, that he doubted the wisdom of his choice.

It was plain to Horton that Duncan was now in serious trouble, not only in the eyes of the law, but also in terms of survival. The wood from the broken canteens told him that the kid had a water problem, and no Texan ever gave up his saddle if he wasn't desperate. The lawman knew that there was supposed to be water in a canyon southwest of there, perhaps a two-hour ride away. On foot the journey would take closer to twice as long. But it was getting dark, and Horton thought that he might just camp here and start again at first light.

The sheriff piled Duncan's gear and his own in a sheltered spot under a cedar, and after sharing his water with his horse, he set out to take one last look at the signs. The light was almost gone when he stopped as though he had been pole-axed. For there in the dirt was the unmistakable print of an unshod hoof, following Duncan's trail. Horton's heart thumped as he realized instantly that Duncan now had two people on his trail—himself and a Comanche warrior. He hoped for Duncan's sake that he found the kid before the Comanche did.

Yellow Horse was eager, but he was not foolish. He rode swiftly but carefully from his father's camp back to the spot where he had last seen Swift Eagle. Then he had ridden in a large circle, cutting the man's back trail. He saw a man coming along the trail, but at his present speed he would take hours to come abreast of the spot from which Yellow Horse watched. The warrior noted that the roan horse that the white man rode would make a fine mount for himself, or perhaps a suitable trade for the hand of Owl Song, the woman who drove him nearly mad with only a glance from the corner of her eye.

The Indian moved cautiously until he was sure that the lone rider could not see him, then he rode a path parallel to the route taken by Swift Eagle. He saw without stopping where his adopted brother and his horse had fallen, and he knew at that moment that he had only to ride to the spring in the Canyon With Eyes to find his quarry.

It was said that spirits lived in the canyon, guarding all who entered there. It was a haven for all who traveled within its walls, and even the deadliest of enemies must share the water and the hospitality of the place or risk offending the spirits. The abundant game was safe in the canyon, too, for no blood of any kind could be shed there without arousing the wrath of the guardian spirits.

Yellow Horse scoffed at the legend, but he was a little uneasy, too. He thought that just possibly there might be some basis to the stories, but he set his jaw in determination to put the legend to the test. He would capture Swift Eagle tonight or kill him if capture were not possible. The spirits could do as they wished after that. Then it would be too late. Even if the spirits killed him, his memory would be honored as the slayer of Swift Eagle. His name and story would be sung around the campfires of his people for generations to come. If Yellow Horse had a concept of immortality, this would have been it.

Tommy Duncan was tired. He was hot, his water was gone, and every muscle in his legs and back protested against this forced march. The sun was nearly a memory, a huge orange glow on the western horizon where he entered the canyon where he had been assured by the Comanche that a spring would be found. He remembered, too, the stories of the guardian spirits, and he decided to honor the legend. He would take only water and any berries or roots he could find before he started on his way in the morning.

He found the spring about a half mile up the canyon, under the northern rim. There were trees there, and firewood, too, left by those who had passed before him. There were many paths cut in the grass by animals headed for water. Duncan chose a camp site about fifty yards from the spring, under the trees and away from the canyon wall where snakes might lurk. He built a small fire to discourage animal visitors, then went to the spring, where he drank and filled his canteen. He went back to his camp, spread his ground sheet, rolled up in his blanket and fell instantly into a sound sleep. He never heard the animals who visited the spring to water, and he knew nothing of the eyes that peered at him out of the darkness. He did not sense the shadow that detached itself from among those of the trees and moved stealthily toward him as he slept, nor did he hear the knife as it was drawn from its sheath so that its blade could glitter dully in the light of the moon.

Slowly the shadow crept closer, soundlessly covering the distance to the sleeping man. As the figure came closer, light from the dying fire illuminated the back eyes of the man with the knife, revealing the depths of the hatred to be found within the man. The figure came closer. Duncan slept.

Chapter 6

It was nearly two hours after he had been tied to his horse and led away before Jack regained consciousness. His broken nose and hand, combined with his enforced head-down position during his ride had given him a terrible headache. He moaned softly and then shook his head to clear it. Discovering that his head would not fall off, he risked opening first one eye and then the other. He was rewarded for his efforts with a new surge of pain and a sudden, uncontrollable nausea. He vomited until he was sure that he must have thrown up his toenails, then he called out weakly.

"Harry! Marco! Stop this damned horse!"

Marco heard Jack and wondered what he should do. He looked back and saw that Harry was beginning to stir, too, but Marco had problems of his own. The stumps of his broken teeth were killing him. For the last two hours he had been trying to get up enough nerve to turn Jack's horse loose, and him with it. Now it was too late. Marco feared Jack, with or without his guns. The Mississippi bottom farm of his childhood seemed very far off at the moment.

"Marco, I said to stop this damned horse and I meant it!" Jack shouted in a stronger voice.

The decision point was passed. Marco stopped the horses.

Marco got off his horse and ran back to Jack. Swiftly he untied the young tough, then he helped him to the ground. Jack swayed slightly, took a couple of steps, and then folded abruptly in the middle and was wracked by spasms of dry heaves. Marco took the opportunity to go over to his brother Harry and untie him, too. Harry moaned as Marco eased him to the ground, then sat up and tried to focus his eyes. He quickly thought better of the idea and lay back down and closed his eyes.

Jack finally straightened and walked back to his horse. He reached for his canteen and was suddenly reminded that his right hand was smashed. Somehow, he got the stopper out and raised the canteen to his lips. He rinsed his mouth to rid himself of the vomit, then took a couple of long swallows. He felt a little better.

Jack's hand was badly broken, and the swelling had made it look like five very crooked sausages stuffed into a green and purple ball. Jack nearly passed out a couple of times as Marco straightened broken bones. After Marco was satisfied that the ends of the bones were as joined as he'd ever be likely to get them, he went over to Jack's bedroll and pawed through the stuff in there until he found an old shirt. Marco tore the shirt into strips as he walked back to Jack, then sat down and tried to figure out how he could bandage the hand.

Marco finally took one of the shirt sleeves, wadded it into a ball the size of a small fist, and placed it in what had been the palm of Jack's hand. He carefully molded the broken fingers around the ball and then wrapped strips of cloth around the hand. Marco inspected the results and grunted in satisfaction. As a final touch, he placed the broken hand near Jack's left shoulder and then tied the arm against his chest with the last of the cloth from Jack's shirt.

"Not bad, if I do say so myself," Marco stated with more than a little pride.

"It still hurts like hell," Jack said through clenched teeth, "but I gotta admit that it's better'n it was. You damn near killed me settin' the bones."

"I did the best I could, Jack," Marco whined. "At least you still got a hand. My teeth are gone for good." He peeled up his lip so Jack could see the broken stumps.

Harry moaned and tried to sit up again. This time he made it.

"Where the hell are we?" he finally managed to say.

"We're two hours east of Cedar Station," Marco volunteered. "Not more'n seven, eight miles. I rode slow on account o' you was hurt."

Jack looked at the sun and saw that it was well past noon.

"We're goin' back," Jack said. "We're goin' back an' teach those bastards a lesson."

"Now just how are we goin' to do that?" Marco asked. "We got no guns, you got a busted hand, Harry's got a busted head, an' I don't feel none too good, either."

Jack got to his feet and turned to his partners angrily.

"We're goin' back, I tell you, an' we're gonna make 'em all pay. I don't know how we're gonna do it, but we are gonna try."

"Whatever you want, Jack," Harry said as he sat cross-legged, holding his head in his hands. "I just ain't up to gettin' on no horse right now."

Jack walked over and kicked Harry's leg. Harry let out a howl of protest that brought Marco to his feet.

"You'll do what I tell you if you know what's good for you," Jack snarled at Harry.

"Leave him alone," Marco demanded. "The fact is that neither one of you are fit to ride. Why don't we set up camp an' ride back in the mornin'?"

Jack's eyes narrowed as he fought against this challenge to his authority. It was the first time that anyone had questioned him or his authority, and he didn't like it one bit. But he could not argue with the truth of Marco's argument.

"Maybe we'd better wait a little," Jack conceded. "They won't expect no trouble tomorrow." Then his voice hardened. "But tomorrow we're goin', an' I don't care how you feel. We're goin' back an' there's no more argument."

And there was none.

Later that night, Jack nudged the sleeping Marco awake.

"Wake up, Marco. It's your turn to stand watch."

Marco groaned and sat up, wiping the sleep from his eyes.

"Why bother?" he asked. "We got no guns or nothin'. Why don't we all just go to sleep? We all could use it?"

"Get up!" Jack demanded. "At least you can give a warnin' if someone comes in. We could jump 'em an' get their guns."

Marco got up, took his blanket, and moved away from the fire. He waited until Jack was snoring soundly, then he crept back into camp and nudged his brother Harry awake. Holding a finger to his lips, Marco motioned Harry to join him near the horses.

"Whaddya want?" Harry asked sleepily.

"Get your stuff an' we'll ride out now," Marco replied.

"Why? Where'll we go?" Harry demanded.

"We'll go back home. This is no place for us. Jack's crazy. He's gonna get us both killed!" Marco said vehemently.

"We can't go, Marco. Jack'd only come after us. Besides," Harry said sulkily, "I'd rather die out here than have pa work me to death back there in Mississippi. Now let me go back to sleep. My head still hurts."

Marco stood there in the shadows, thinking about what he should do next. Finally, he picked up his saddle and the rest of his gear and walked over to the horses. Minutes later he was riding east, back to his home. His pa might thrash him for leaving his brother behind, but if he stayed, that crazy Jack would get them all killed. Besides, he knew something that the others didn't. He had heard the sheriff say that he'd kill them on sight if he ever saw them again.

Marco believed the sheriff.

Miles away, Claire Duncan paced the floor of her living room. Her eyes were red and puffy. She had been crying again, something she had been doing steadily for nearly a week now.

She heard a knock at her door, so she walked across the room and opened it a crack. She saw Rufus Pflugg standing there on the porch. She opened the door and let him in.

"Sorry to bother you at this time of night, my dear," the mayor said, "but I saw your light and thought that I'd see if you were all right."

"That was very kind of you, Mr. Mayor," she said as she daintily wiped a tear from the corner of her eye.

"I'm going as well as I can expect, given the circumstances."

"Call me Rufus, my dear," the mayor said as he moved over to her and put his arm around her shoulders. "I'd like to help you in any way I can."

"Thank you, Mr. Mayor—Rufus, but there is nothing you can do. Tommy was part of that awful gang that killed poor Mr. Swenson. He's wanted for murder! If they catch him, he'll hang!" she exclaimed and then began to sob uncontrollably.

"There, there, my dear," Pflugg said as he took Claire into his arms. He felt her body press against his and his pulse quickened. "Things have a way of working themselves out. Perhaps the sheriff won't be able to catch him."

"But he will!" the woman cried. "Damn Matt Horton and his misplaced sense of duty!" She sobbed as she drew away from the mayor, who reluctantly released his hold on her. "He'll catch Tommy and bring him back to hang! I just know he will!"

"If he does, perhaps I could do something for you," the mayor suggested. "I'm not without influence, you know."

Clair wiped her eyes and looked up at the mayor.

"But what could you do?" she asked. "And why would you want to help Tommy? You never trusted him after he came back from living with the Comanches."

"I'm sure that you exaggerate, my dear," the mayor said as he attempted to take Claire into his arms. "I always thought highly of the boy."

Claire took a step back and looked questioningly at the mayor.

"Are you suggesting that you could help Tommy if we came to some sort of ... of arrangement?" she asked.

"I'm sure that we could work out something, my dear," the mayor said as he took a step closer.

The mayor's advance was met by a roundhouse right from Claire. The blow struck the mayor full on the left cheek and dislodged his glasses. He caught them before they hit the floor and put them back on with all the dignity that he could muster.

"There must be some misunderstanding," he said as he backed away from the irate woman. "I only meant ...."

"You only meant that you'd trade Tommy's life for my virtue. There was no misunderstanding, Mr. Mayor. Now get out of my house before I feel a need to talk with Mrs. Pflugg!"

"Now Claire, don't do anything hasty," the mayor said as he opened the door. "I never meant ...."

"Git!" Claire exclaimed, "And don't come back!"

Rufus Pflugg got.

Claire sat down in a chair and started once more to sob, but very quickly the sobs changed to a throaty laugh.

"I guess it wouldn't have been much of a trade, anyway," she said to herself as she wiped away the last of her tears. "Matt Horton got my virtue months ago."

She thought of the contest being waged between her brother and her lover and wondered how she would ever be able to love the victor again.

Chapter 7

Tommy Duncan sensed rather than saw the shadow move stealthily towards him. At first, he thought that it must be the sheriff, but the shadow was too slight, and besides, this wasn't the way Horton would try to take him. So, the young outlaw lay still as the shadow came ever closer.

The fire had burned down to coals and cast only a little light, but what there was proved to be more than enough for Tommy. Through the slits of his eyes, he could see the shadow take form. Tommy saw the dull gleam of the raised knife, and he clutched his own Army model Colt a little tighter in his hand as he waited.

Tommy moved his eyes ever so slightly, searching the shadows for other deadly forms, but he saw none. This whole situation is impossible, he thought, one lone Comanche would not be doing this, not at night and certainly not in the Canyon With Eyes. But he knew that he was not dreaming. The crouched figure, poised to strike, was very real and quite deadly.

As Tommy watched, the figure seemed to coil tighter, and then with a blood-curdling cry, it leaped!

The outlaw rolled to his left and felt the tug of the blade as it snagged a piece of his shirt. Tommy swung the Colt in an arc and felt it connect, but not solidly. He heard the Comanche grunt with pain and then the two figures were rolling together on the ground, each seeking an advantage over the other.

Duncan found himself on his back, the Indian poised above him. He felt the Comanche take a vice-like grip on his right wrist, preventing him from bringing the big Colt to bear. As he saw the knife descend for the fatal blow, Tommy managed to grip the Comanche's wrist and deflect the thrust. He heard the Indian grunt in despair, and then they were rolling again, locked in mortal combat.

Still clutching the other's wrist, the two men somehow managed to get to their feet. The Comanche started to pivot, the move taken to throw the young outlaw over his hip and into eternity. Duncan read the move and countered with a vicious knee to the warrior's groin.

The Indian groaned in pain and Tommy felt the grip on his wrist relax slightly. It was enough to allow him to break the warrior's grip and bring the Colt into firing position. Even as he thumbed back the hammer, he thought better of it and lashed out instead, laying the barrel of the pistol alongside the Comanche's head with enough force to fell a mule.

The Indian crumpled to the ground without a sound. Duncan crouched over the unconscious form, searching the darkness for others who might be lurking nearby, ready to try their hand at killing him. He waited silently for several minutes, but nothing moved. Nothing happened at all. Duncan finally decided that, as incredible as it seemed, this one warrior who lay at his feet had acted alone.

Finally, Duncan reached down and took hold of the Comanche's braids and dragged him close to the fire. The young outlaw threw more wood on the coals and tied the warrior's hands behind his back as the flames took hold of the wood. After thinking about it for a moment, he tied the Indian's feet, too, then he rolled the still-unconscious form onto his back.

The flames from the fire had risen considerably, and the flickering light was more than enough to illuminate the features of the captive. Duncan gasped in recognition. Although he had not laid eyes upon him for more than three years, he recognized his blood brother Yellow Horse immediately even under the war paint that covered his face.

Now the young outlaw was really confused. It was hard enough to understand this attack in the first place, but he could not understand why this warrior, the boy with whom he had hunted and fished and played pranks, would try to kill him. The Comanche weren't even at war, at least not to his knowledge.

Why, unless the Indian had not recognized him. Duncan quickly discarded that possibility. The attack was too deliberate, too well-planned for the warrior not to have recognized him. He had changed as little as Yellow Horse.

The young outlaw sat back and tried to think of some logical answer. He was no closer to a solution to his question than when he started, and the Indian wasn't going to be in any shape to answer questions for some time. He decided to stash the warrior for the night so he could get some sleep himself.

Duncan took hold of the length of rope that was left over from tying the warrior's feet and dragged the man over to a tree. He threw the rope over a low limb and pulled until the man's heels were about two feet off the ground. He tied the rope off around the trunk of the tree and then inspected the results.

"It'd take a better man than you to get loose from that," he said to the unconscious form. "You may not like it, but you'll still be there come sunup."

Duncan went back to the fire, threw the Indian's knife into the night, and then rolled up in his blanket again, his Colt clutched in his fist. He was asleep before the flames of the fire started to die down.

Dawn found Jack kicking Harry awake and cussing a blue streak.

"Wake up, you ... you ...." In his anger, Jack could not find the words he wanted. "Your lousy brother's gone, an' he took one of the horses with him. Where'd he go?" he demanded.

Harry rolled away from Jack's battering foot and got to his feet. He staggered a couple of steps as if he were drunk, then managed to gain his balance. He shook his head in an unsuccessful attempt to clear it, then he blinked his eyes a couple of times and tried to focus on Jack. He didn't have much luck with that, either. And he still had the headache, even worse than before, if that could be possible.

"What are you talkin' about?" Harry finally managed to ask. "Where's Marco?"

"That's what I'm askin' you, you fool!" Jack raged. "Where'd that back-stabbin' brother of yours go?"

"I don't know, Jack," the man said as he walked over to a fallen tree and sat down. "Maybe he went after somethin' for us to eat."

"Not very damned likely," Jack answered. "The closest place is Cedar Station, an' he wouldn't go back there alone. Are you sure that he didn't say nuthin' to you about lightin' out?"

"He didn't say nuthin' to me," Harry lied. Suddenly he turned aside and retched.

"I don't feel too good," he added unnecessarily.

Jack fumed, but there wasn't much that he could do about the way things were. His belly rumbled with hunger, and he searched his saddlebags for something to eat. He found nothing there, so he went through Harry's saddlebags as well. His search was rewarded with a can of peaches. Jack looked over at Harry, but the other man wasn't paying him any attention.

"He'd only heave 'em up anyway," Jack muttered to himself as he tried to open the can with his knife. It was a tough job using only one hand, and before he was done, he had tipped the can over several times, losing most of the juice and half of the peaches in the process. Once he'd eaten the rest, his mood improved a little.

"Harry, come over here and help me saddle this horse," Jack demanded. "An' you better saddle your own while you're at it. We're goin' after that worthless brother of yours."

Harry shuffled over to the horses, still moving as if he were drunk. Between the two of them they finally got Jack's horse saddled, but the effort had clearly done in Harry. He seemed ready to collapse.

Jack went over and looked at the other man. One pupil was twice the size of the other, and there was a knot the size of a goose egg where he had been hit the day before. Jack wasn't sure but what Harry might be dying, and for some reason that scared him a little.

"I think you'd better stay here in case Marco is out after food an' comes back," Jack said.

"I ain't gonna argue with you," Harry replied weakly. "I'm sure enough wore out. Think I'm gonna turn in again."

"Jack watched the man curl up in his bedroll, then he mounted his horse and headed east, following Marco's trail.

It wasn't long before Jack decided to untie his arm for a while. It was pretty sore, and he thought that moving it around some might help. He looped the reins around the saddle horn and untied the strips of cloth that held his right arm against his chest. Nothing much happened when he flexed it, but he nearly passed out when he lowered the arm to his side and the blood rushed to his shattered hand. He had never felt such intense pain in his whole life, and he cursed the man at the bar who was sure had stomped him after he was down.

Jack managed to stay in the saddle and get his arm raised again, but the damage had been done. He lost all interest in following Marco. As far as the rider was concerned, he had wasted enough time and energy on the other man. He also had lost some of his interest in returning to Cedar Station, at least right away. He decided that a few more days in camp wouldn't hurt anything, especially if they were able to find something to eat. He managed to turn his horse around and headed back.

When Jack finally got into camp, he found that he and Harry were no longer alone. Two riders had joined Harry, and coffee was boiling at the fire. Jack's stomach rumbled at the smell.

The two new riders stood up when Jack dismounted. Jack thought about jumping them for their guns and whatever else they had, then gave up the idea as a bad one. He'd have a hard time handling a ten-year-old in his present condition, and he couldn't count on Harry for any help at all.

One of the new riders, who seemed the friendly sort, walked over to Jack and spoke.

"Your friend here didn't say much, but from the looks of him an' you, 'pears to me you've had some trouble."

"Yeah," Jack answered, "we got jumped yesterday. Somebody stole our whole damn outfit. Harry over there may be dyin', an' I ain't too well off, either. What's more, I'm so hungry that I could eat the north end of a southbound skunk. You fellas wouldn't have any extra food, would you?"

The first rider looked at his partner and then back to Jack. They'd ridden around the camp before they'd ridden in and had seen no sign of a fight. From the signs, though, there'd been a third man in the camp. The rider mentioned that to Jack.

"You're right as rain," Jack replied. "We had another man along, an' it may have been him that done us in. We was asleep an' then the next thing you know, why, we're here, all busted up an' he's long gone, an' all our stuff, too."

The rider thought about that for a while and then decided that he wouldn't push it any further. Something about Jack's story didn't ring true, but it wasn't any of his business.

"We're headed for the tradin' post at Cedar Station," the rider said. "We'd take you with us, but your partner here ain't fit to ride. You can have whatever chuck we got left. Sorry that we can't help you out none with any guns. We need what few we got."

Jack thanked the men and watched them stack the food next to Harry. There was part of a side of bacon, past its prime and a little rancid but still edible, some dried beans, some jerky, a little coffee, an onion, and a little hard tack. Jack guessed that there was enough food in the pile for two or three days if they were careful, maybe more if Harry died.

"I got nuthin' to pay you with," Jack said. "The rat got all our cash, too."

"Wasn't expectin' no pay," the rider who had been doing the talking said. "You'd do the same for us, was the situation reversed."

Jack doubted that, but he wasn't about to argue. He thanked them again and waved as the two men mounted and rode out of camp.

"Wish I coulda got ahold of a gun," Jack muttered under his breath as he lost sight of the riders.

"Damn glad that jasper didn't have a gun," the first rider said to his partner. "He looks like a hard case to me."

His partner nodded in agreement and slipped the Derringer that he'd been holding back into his boot. He hadn't trusted the busted-paw man, either. He thought of telling that to his partner but gave up on the idea.

That's the trouble with this world, he thought. Too damn much talk.

They rode on in silence.

Chapter 8

Tommy Duncan was up and ready to ride when the first light crept into the eastern sky. It had not taken him very long to find Yellow Horse's mount. He had walked toward the mouth of the canyon, crooning softly as he had learned to do while he lived with the Comanche, and the horse had nickered back. Duncan was glad that the animal was more friendly than its rider.

And the rider's attitude had not improved over the hours that he had lain trussed up to the tree, either. His black eyes glittered with hate, and he absolutely refused to answer any of Duncan's questions. He just laid there, looking up at Duncan, willing that the Anglo youth would die.

Duncan tried again, talking in Comanche so that there would be no chance that Yellow Horse would misunderstand.

"My brother, why did you come here to kill me?" he asked, kneeling close to the Indian. "I have done nothing to you or our people, and this is a sacred place. Why have you risked offending the spirits?"

"I am not your brother!" Yellow Horse hissed. "As for the rest of what you say, my reasons are my own."

"Where are Spotted Calf and Running Buffalo? Are they close by to see your dishonor?" Duncan asked.

But Yellow Horse would say no more.

Duncan was caught between a rock and a hard place. He couldn't kill Yellow Horse as he laid there, and to leave him tied to that tree was to kill him, only more slowly. Matt Horton might find him; then again, he might not. To turn the Indian loose was just not the smart thing to do. Yellow Horse would beat his brains out with a stick if he got half a chance. And there was no way that Duncan was going to take the young warrior with him. That would be like trying to kiss a rattler on the lips. Time was running out. He must be on his way in a matter of minutes. Horton would not linger over his morning coffee.

Duncan stood up and drew his knife from the scabbard at his side. Yellow Horse's eyes widened a little, surprise showing briefly on his face. Then the hate was back in his eyes and in his voice as he spoke.

"You are learning, Swift Eagle. You must kill me now or I will surely kill you later."

"Brother, you're gonna have to try a whole lot harder than you did last night or you're never goin' to get the job done," he said in English, which he knew Yellow Horse understood, but he repeated it in Comanche, just to make sure.

Yellow Horse said nothing, but Duncan could tell that his words had shamed him. He struggled with his ropes, then lay still.

Duncan thought of untying the rope from the tree and then thought better of the idea. He cut Yellow Horse's feet free instead, and quickly dodged a kick sent his way as a reward. Duncan stopped down and scooped up a handful of loose dirt and threw it in the Indian's face. The effect could not have been greater if Duncan had thrown him in the river.

Yellow Horse spit and sputtered as he tried to blink the dirt and tears from his eyes and mouth. He had expected to be killed, but he had been cut loose instead. He had hoped that his kick would provide a bullet that would save him from the shame of returning empty-handed to his father. Instead, he had gotten a handful of dirt in the face. In that moment his resolve cracked.

"Running Buffalo is dead!" he spat. Suddenly he realized what he had said, what was implied, and his mouth shut like a steel trap.

"I'm sorry to hear that," Duncan said sincerely. A light suddenly dawned in him. "And you think that I did it, is that what this is all about?"

But Yellow Horse had recovered his composure and would not speak again.

"Because if that's what you think, my brother, then you're wrong. Dead wrong! I would never have done anything to hurt or shame my adopted brothers and father."

Duncan stood and watched the Indian for any indication that he had believed or even heard him, but he saw none. Time was getting short, so he grabbed the warrior by the arm and pulled him to his feet. Yellow Horse twisted away from him, then stood, glaring defiantly.

"Think what you want, Yellow Horse," Duncan said finally. "I'm taking your horse. A man is following me that I do not want to meet. You will have to walk back to your village. For your sake, I hope that it is not far. I am sorry, but I must leave your hands tied to make sure that we do not fight again."

Duncan went over to the horse and mounted. Looking down at Yellow Horse, he said, "Listen carefully. Let this foolishness end here. I did not harm your brother, and I wish you no harm. But if you ever attack me again, you will no longer be my brother and I will kill you. That would bring greater sadness to your father's heart."

Yellow Horse looked up at him and spat.

Duncan wheeled his horse and rode from the Canyon With Eyes.

Matt Horton wasted no time that morning, either. He was back on the trail as soon as there was light enough to see the sign. He saw the unshod hoof prints that followed the tracks made by the young fugitive, and he wondered again what was going on.

His load was heavier that day because he had taken the kid's cache with him. When the sheriff caught up with the kid, they'd look for another mount for the outlaw, and the saddle would make the ride easier, even though Horton knew that Duncan was perfectly at ease aboard a bare-backed, unbroken mustang. Maybe he was getting soft, he thought, or maybe he was just trying to ease his conscience. Anyway, he had the kid's gear with him, and he hoped that Duncan would soon have a chance to use it.

It took the sheriff two hours to reach the mouth of the canyon. He dismounted there to look at the sign. He saw old sign, made last night, where one man wearing moccasins and one unshod pony had entered the canyon. There were fresh tracks, too, that showed the unshod pony headed to the south and east, and the set of moccasin tracks headed north. The sheriff puzzled over that for a while. Why should the two sets of tracks that had followed each other so closely yesterday separate at the mouth of the canyon today? It didn't make sense. Something else was wrong, too. For six days Duncan had never deviated from the most direct route to El Paso. Now neither set of tracks were headed in that direction. What was going on?

Horton thought about it as he walked along, following the fresh moccasin prints. They wandered from side to side, and no attempt had been made to hide them.

Horton suddenly stopped dead in his tracks. There in front of him was unmistakable sign that a man had stumbled and fallen to his knees.

"Maybe they fought back there in the canyon an' Duncan's hurt," he said softly. But try as hard as he could, he could find no trace of blood, and the tracks led north.

Horton mounted his horse and followed the man on foot.

Yellow Horse was furious. He plodded along, unable to avoid all of the branches from the low-growing mesquite bushes and the cedar. He tried twisting and tugging at the ropes that bound his wrists behind his back, but he had succeeded only in chafing his wrists to the point where they bled. Sweat from his exertions ran down his arms and into his wounds, making them even more painful.

He had traveled for more than two hours before he found an outcropping of rock that looked promising. There was a lot of jagged stone there that looked sharp enough and strong enough to cut through the ropes that added further insult to his dignity. He worked and strained for nearly half an hour before the ropes parted and he was free again. He had cut himself badly and there was much blood, but he felt no pain now that he was free.

He wanted to turn south, to follow Swift Eagle and kill him. He knew that over the course of a day or two a warrior on foot could easily outdistance a horse. But there were other problems. He had no knife or weapon of any kind, and his quarry had said that he would kill him if he was attacked again. Yellow Horse was not afraid of the youth, but he knew that to stand a chance against Swift Eagle he needed a weapon, something more than a rock and a hatred that could not be quenched.

Reluctantly, then, Yellow Horse turned again in the direction of his village and began to run. He would get his weapons, he would get a horse, and he would get his man. He promised that to himself.

When Horton got to the outcropping of rock where Yellow Horse had cut himself free, he dismounted and studied the sign. There was blood—a lot of it, dried now and being feasted upon by insects. There were pieces of rope, too. Now the sheriff knew why the tracks had been so strange. The man had been off-balance because his hands had been tied behind his back! And the tracks had changed. The man was running now, running in this land of great heat and little water. Different Tommy Duncan might be—strange, even—but crazy he was not. Matt Horton knew now beyond all doubt that he had been following a false trail. A Comanche warrior may have ridden into that canyon, but it had been Tommy Duncan who had ridden out, and when he had ridden out, he had changed direction. He was not headed for El Paso. He could be going any-where now. And Horton was seven, maybe eight hours behind him.

The sheriff cursed himself for being a fool and re-mounted his horse. He turned the animal south and urged him into a ground-eating run. The big roan leaped forward eagerly, sensing his rider's urgency. As he backtracked, Horton knew that he should have checked the canyon. He would have known then of the switch in riders. His one assumption had cost him most of a day.

He feared that it also might have cost him the race.

Chapter 9

M att Horton rode as hard as he could without in-
juring his horse. Had he been riding anything but
the roan, he would have had to slow his pace, but the
animal forged ahead, eager to be in the chase. The sheriff threw caution aside. He could not afford to take the
time necessary to scan the country ahead of him for
signs of danger as long as the trail was so clear. He
pulled his Winchester from the scabbard under his leg
and rode with it across the pommel, hoping that he
would be able to react fast enough if he rode headlong
into trouble.

The trail back to the canyon was clear enough, and
Duncan had made no attempt to conceal the tracks
leading to the southeast, at least not at first. The
ground, however, was becoming more broken the closer
the trail came to the Rio Grande, and there were larger
expanses of open rock where the unshod hooves of the
Indian pony had left no mark at all. It wasn't the need
for security but rather the roughness of the terrain and
the scarcity or absence of sign that caused the sheriff
to slow his pursuit.

Another problem was growing, too. The sky was darkening and the wind was picking up, gusting enough for the sheriff to consider tying his hat to his head. The wind was beginning to become laden with fine particles of sand that got in his eyes and mouth and chafed under his clothing. The big roan was bothered by the sand, too. But worst of all, the sand was beginning to wipe out what little sign the fleeing outlaw had left. Horton knew that if Duncan changed his course again, only a miracle would prevent him from losing the kid.

Horton crested a small hill and started down the other side when, not more than twenty feet in front of him, three riders pulled out of the mesquite and onto the trail, facing him. Horton jerked his horse to a stop and thumbed back the hammer of the Winchester.

"Where you go in such a big hurry, señor," the man in the middle called out.

Horton said nothing in reply but looked the men over closely.

The riders facing him were dark and swarthy, with long, rank black hair, drooping moustaches, and wide sombreros. Bandoliers of ammunition crossed their chests and each of the riders carried at least one pistol in his belt and a Spencer repeating carbine resting on his leg. The man who had spoken and who seemed to be the leader had a face that was badly pox-marked. These men were Comancheros, outlaws and renegades who operated on both sides of the border. They were dangerous men, and Horton watched them carefully.

"Hey, señor! No hablas Ingles?" the leader shouted. Then in English he said, "Why you no answer me?" When he grinned, he displayed a mouth full of yellow, uneven teeth.

Horton sat on his horse and said nothing. He let his eyes sweep the bushes on either side of the trail. He could see no one else, but he knew that others could be there, waiting to kill him. More reliable were the reactions of his horse. The roan's ears were forward, and he was looking directly at the trio in front of him. Horton hoped that if there were others the horse would be looking in their direction.

Suddenly the leader thumbed back the big side hammer on his Spencer, and it was too late to wonder who might still be in the mesquite or what might be the best thing to do.

Horton fired his Winchester, then dropped it as he drew his Colt and charged.

Yellow Horse was tired when he reached the Comanche camp, but he pulled himself erect and tried to walk with dignity and as much disdain as he could muster for the curious glances of the other members of the tribe. He was not popular with the other warriors of the tribe, partly because of his vicious temper and partly because of his unwillingness to treat others as his equals. During his absence the story of his mission of honor had spread, and now his enemies and detractors were having a good time over his obvious failure.

"Yellow Horse," one warrior shouted, "Where is your prisoner? Where are your weapons? Where is your horse?"

"That is not Yellow Horse," another offered. "That is Horse Killer. See how he hates to ride."

"That is not the warrior Yellow Horse or even the boy Horse Killer," a third observed loudly. "That is Squaw Who Gets Lost in the Dark!"

Laughter followed him through the camp. A piece of horse manure hit him in the back, and suddenly he found that he was being pelted with those smelly missiles from all directions. He felt completely and utterly humiliated.

But if he thought that he had been used cruelly by those who had followed him to his father's tepee, it was nothing when compared to the reception he received from Spotted Calf.

"I heard your coming long ago," the man said from his seat on a pile of soft robes. He made no gesture for his son to join him.

"To you I gave the honor of avenging the death of your older brother. You had only to capture a boy younger than yourself. You could even have killed him. But instead, you come back to this village like the coyote, a coward with your tail between your legs. Your horse and your weapons and your honor are gone, taken by the one you were sent to bring to me. Now the old women laugh at you openly, not even trying to hide their contempt for you. You have brought not honor but shame to yourself and to me."

"My father ...," Yellow Horse began.

"Do not speak of me in that way," Spotted Calf interrupted angrily. "I am not the father of a coyote, or a coward!"

"Honored One," Yellow Horse began again, "I would like to tell you what happened and I seek your wise counsel. Will you grant me that?"

"Can you offer any excuse for your failure?"

"I cannot, Honored One," the young warrior answered. "I can only ask for your wisdom so that I may try again until either I succeed or my spirit leaves my body."

Spotted Calf got to his feet and approached his disgraced son.

"You have often tried, Yellow Horse, and you have often failed. Your brother Running Buffalo was a good hunter and a brave warrior. He was liked and respected by everyone in the tribe. But others look for you to fail and are disappointed if by some chance you succeed. You have no friends here. Your bad temper and proud manner have turned away all who might have helped you."

"You always favored Running Buffalo over me!" Yellow Horse exclaimed hotly.

Suddenly the younger man found himself flat on his back, his head ringing and a tremendous pain on the side of his head. He realized slowly that his father had hit him.

"You will not speak again of Running Buffalo. From this time, you are not his brother, and you are not my son. You will gather your possessions and leave this tepee now. We will not speak again unless you find a way to regain your honor and the respect of my people. Now go."

Yellow Horse picked himself up from the ground, grabbed the few possessions that were his, and stalked out of the tepee, hot tears of shame on his cheeks. The village looked empty, for everyone had heard the exchange and no one wanted to share in his disgrace.

Inside the tepee Spotted Calf stood unmoving, his anger changing to sadness. Tears ran freely down his cheeks in mourning for his lost sons. First, he had lost Running Buffalo, then Yellow Horse, and now it was up to him to kill the last of his sons, Swift Eagle.

After a time, he picked up his rifle and walked from his tepee. He called to the warriors of the tribe, and they came from everywhere, rifles and bows in their hands and determination in their eyes.

Spotted Calf told them what they must do, and the warriors ran for their mounts. The Comanche were at war, a whole tribe against a blond-haired youth who in years was a little more than a boy. And anyone who was caught between them would surely die.

Pedro O'Brien swept out the trading post, then began closing the shutters over the windows. A storm was in the air, a wind that would probably bring more sand than water to what was even in the best of times a parched land. Pedro never liked to see the storms, for they usually brought predators, both the four-legged and the two-legged variety, who sought shelter within the confines of the trading post and stage station. This time would be no different except for one thing.

This time, Pedro was alone.

Pedro's wife and his hired man had gone north with the wagons to purchase more supplies and to renegotiate the stage contract. Pedro had no head for business, but his wife was as sharp as they come. They had long ago decided that he would handle the selling, and she would take care of all contracts, purchasing, and bargaining. It was a happy arrangement, except for times like these, when Pedro became sad and often sought the comfort of his liquid merchandise.

Although the hour was still early, the sky was darkening rapidly. Pedro lit the lamps in the station, then went outside to take care of the horses. He moved Horton's grey and the horse Tommy Duncan had traded into the barn and left the mustangs in the corral. He watered and fed all of the stock, then made his way back to the station, dodging tumbleweeds and other flying objects as he went. He saw a dark blur enter the stone corral and decided that a coyote or some such animal had already found shelter from the storm.

He closed the door to the station behind him and listened to the wind begin to howl. He went behind the bar and dusted off a bottle of Irish Whiskey, the brand that had been such a favorite of first his father and now of himself.

He, too, had found shelter from the storm.

Chapter 10

Bartholemew "Bart the Bastard" Beaudreaux traveled south along the trail that led to the Rio Grande and safety. He carried his saddle on his back and his Winchester in his hand, staggering from time to time under the load as the rising storm and fatigue took their toll. He didn't look back. He didn't need to. All that lay behind him was a dead stage driver, a posse, and a rope. His horse was back there someplace, too, ridden to death in his attempt to escape the quick justice that would be his fate if he were caught.

Bart cursed the sand as it sifted through the bandana that he had tied across his face, but at the same time it would be filling his tracks behind him, making the job of the posse more difficult or even impossible. He resented the fact that they could afford to hole up for the duration of the storm while he must keep on, storm or no storm. If he stopped, he would be caught, and he knew it.

Coming over a rise, Bart saw that the trail he was following merged with another headed southeast. He dumped his saddle at the edge of the brush and sat where he could watch the trail as he tried to catch his breath. The wind was coming almost directly from the west, bringing with it enough dust, sand, leaves, and other debris to nearly block out the sun.

The outlaw sat there a while, trying to decide what to do. This new trail probably would take him east to Eagle Pass or west to El Paso, he thought. He tried to put himself in the mind of the posse. Eagle Pass was closer—much closer. The posse would expect him to go there. He still had some water, and he had a little food, too. He decided to take the longer route to El Paso. He counted on the storm erasing all traces of his passes.

Bart kicked his saddle under a cedar, picked up his rifle, and started walking into the wind. Almost immediately he began to regret his decision. He could not keep his eyes open to the wind for more than a few moments. The wind tore at his clothing and made walking extremely difficult. After a few minutes he stopped, turned his back to the wind and looked back to where he had started. His breath was labored and his lungs were on fire from his efforts and from the dirt that found its way into his mouth and nose. Worse yet, when he looked back, he saw that he had covered fewer than two hundred yards.

Bart sat down again in the brush, just back from the trail. He thought that he might stay there a while, at least until the wind dropped a little. He considered rolling himself a smoke and then put the thought from his mind. He'd never get it lit. He cursed for the hundredth time and tried to make himself into a smaller figure, less vulnerable to the wind.

It was only a few minutes before he heard a noise coming from the west, carried by the wind. Bart recognized the sound as that of hooves on a patch of loose shale. He strained his ears to hear more. Had the posse cut the trail in another place, or was this something or someone else? His mind tried to draw conclusions from what he heard, and then the sound was gone, either stopped or carried away by the wind.

The outlaw stretched out on the ground, rifle at his shoulder, waiting impatiently for the rider or riders to come into view. He wiped the sand and the tears from his eyes and tried to concentrate on the trail, but the wind made concentration difficult. He decided to let whatever was coming along the trail ride past him. He could then shoot with the wind and sand at his back. Let anyone who tried to return his fire try to shoot straight with sand in his eyes.

Bart checked his rifle again after he had shifted his position to better cover his back trail. He heard again the sound of hooves on shale, and this time the sound was distinct enough for him to decide that there was only a single rider. He also knew what he had not heard. He had not heard the sound of iron on stone. The horse was unshod. It was either wild or an Indian mount. The outlaw smiled under his bandana.

Either way, he meant to have that horse.

Tommy Duncan rode steadily to the southwest along the trail he had found shortly after he had left the canyon that morning. The storm was covering his tracks well enough, he knew, but he would soon leave the trail and head due south until he reached the Rio Grande. If Horton was still on his trail, he would probably miss the turn off and stay with the trail, assuming that he, Tommy, would follow it through Eagle Pass into Mexico. By following the river, Duncan thought that he could find a good ford, cross into Mexico, and bypass Eagle Pass altogether. The plan had merit, he thought, and for the first time in a week he thought that he just might live long enough to see another birthday. He smiled to himself as he rode, thinking of his sister Claire and how happy she'd be when he finally wrote to her that he was safe.

Duncan crested a small hill and stopped about halfway down the other side, finding a little shelter from the wind. About three hundred yards to his front he saw where another trail joined the one that he followed. He saw no strange movement, but even as he searched, he knew that his vigilance was useless. The wind would cover any movement in the brush.

The hairs on the back of the young outlaw's neck prickled and sent a chill down his spine. Something was wrong. He sensed it, but he did not know what it was. The pony he rode plodded on, more concerned with the wind than with anything else. Duncan held his rifle in one hand as he reined his horse along the trail, alert for the trouble that he knew was there but which he could not see.

Duncan heard the rifle crack behind him and felt a violent blow on the side of his head. Everything turned black, but he did not pass out immediately. He felt himself slipping from the back of his horse and he tried to hold on, but the animal smelled the blood from his wound and began to buck. Duncan was thrown from his horse into the brush.

Tommy knew that he was hurt, maybe even dying, but he was determined not to be taken easily. He crawled deeper into the brush, on and on, dragging his Henry with him. His movements became weaker and weaker and then stopped entirely. Tommy Duncan had gone as far as he could.

Bart watched the rider ride past him and was relieved to see that he was little more than a boy. The outlaw waited for the rider to get out of easy pistol range, then rose to one knee, sighted carefully, and squeezed the trigger. The Winchester jumped in his hands, and he saw the rider slump against the horse's neck, struggling to stay on its back. He levered another cartridge into the chamber and prepared for a second shot when the horse freed itself from the rider and took off at a run down the trail.

Bart was faced with something of a problem. He wanted to find the rider in the brush and finish him off, and he wanted to catch that horse and ride swiftly away from the posse at his heels. His need for the horse finally proved greater than his need to kill the rider. The outlaw got to his feet and began chasing the animal.

The horse ran only a short way before it decided that the danger had passed. It slowed its pace to walk and finally stopped near the trail junction. Soon afterward Bart came upon the horse. After a few spoiled attempts, the outlaw managed to snag a rein and the chase was over.

Bart led the horse to the place where he had left his saddle. In less time than it takes to tell about it, the outlaw had the animal saddled and was riding toward Eagle Pass. Bart changed his mind and decided to take his chances with the posse now that he had another horse under him. Besides, he had seen the rider look behind him as he had crested that last hill. He didn't know what the kid was riding away from, but he didn't want to tangle with it, either. So, he rode toward Eagle Pass as fast as he could without killing the horse. He did not want to stretch his luck and find himself afoot again.

Bart Beaudreaux did not have to hurry. The posse that he feared was no longer at his heels. In fact, the

posse had turned back long before Beaudreaux had ridden his horse to death. The stage that the outlaw had
stopped had carried no strongbox or passengers, and
the driver, while dead, was not known to either the
sheriff or to the other members of the posse, so their
pursuit had been half-hearted at best. When the storm
began, the interests of justice had been overcome by
the desire for shelter. The posse lay huddled under
ground sheets while Bart rode away to safety in Mexico.
The posse had never come close enough to the outlaw
to identify him.

Tommy Duncan struggled back to consciousness. His
head throbbed badly, but the bleeding had stopped and
he could see. He tried to stand and found that he could
not, so he crawled slowly back to the edge of the trail.
His bedroll and canteen were tied across his back, since
the Indian pony he had been riding had not been saddled. He took a couple of pulls at the canteen and then
wrapped himself in his ground sheet and sat down to
wait for the storm to blow itself out.

Duncan knew that he had been lucky. The shot that
had wounded him had been meant to kill. He had been
foolish to ignore his sense of danger, and he vowed that
if he lived through this, he would not ignore it again,
even if Horton was on his trail. He had relearned a valu-
able truth: danger and death came from many direc-

tions, and a man must be alert to each as he traveled through life. If a man were not alert, then the journey would be short.

Matt Horton had been lucky, too. The shot he had fired at the center Comanchero had struck him in the throat, flinging him out of the saddle and over his horse's rump. He lay in the sand, drowning in his own blood.

Horton aimed the big roan at the renegade on the left, drew his Colt, and snapped a shot at the Comanchero on his right. He felt the roan collide with the outlaw's horse and saw it go down with the rider under it. He thumbed back the hammer of his Colt for another shot, but suddenly he was past the trio, without a decent target. He had an urge to hug the roan's neck and light out of there as fast as he could, but reason prevailed and he swung the horse around for another charge.

He rode back but found little left to attack. The leader of the trio was laying in the trail, looking like a soiled bunch of rags. There was no mistaking the fact that he was dead. The second Comanchero at whom he had fired was also dead. Horton's snap shot had caught him in the left eye and had taken out a large part of the back of his head.

"Lucky shot," Horton said to no one in particular. "'Nother half a inch an' I'd of missed him completely." Such was the difference between life and death he mused as he dismounted to check out the third outlaw.

The man snarled as Horton walked over to him. His horse had rolled on him when they fell, and the man's spine was broken somewhere high up, making it impossible for the man to use his arms or anything below.

"Finish it, gringo," the man said between clenched teeth.

Horton looked down at the man and said, "An' you'd of done the same for me, I suppose."

The outlaw coughed wetly and then smiled, revealing a bloody froth on his mouth.

"I watch you die slow, gringo, an' you know it. But I feel nothing now but cold. You cannot hurt me. Finish it now. Maybe I get warm again in hell."

Horton raised the Colt and aimed at the outlaw's head. It would be an act of kindness to finish off the Comanchero, he told himself. Still, he hesitated.

"Finish it!" the outlaw hissed.

Horton fired. It was finished.

Chapter 11

The wind continued to blow throughout the night, but only an occasional drop of rain reached the ground. In spite of the boiling clouds and the flashes of lightning, the earth remained as parched as before. Dawn came and the wind settled. The land seemed to breathe a sigh of relief, and life went on as before.

Matt Horton unwrapped himself from his ground sheet and slowly stood to his full height. Joints popped and cramped muscles protested as he worked out the stiffness that had come from his enforced idleness. He took some jerky from his saddlebags and chewed on it as he checked his water. He found that he still had a canteen and a half, so, using his hat as a bucket, he gave the roan the larger measure and saved the half canteen for himself. He thought that if he didn't find a pool or a spring somewhere that day, he'd have to make a detour to find water. Without water there could be no chase.

Horton would have liked to make coffee, but he did not have the water to waste. But more than coffee, the lawman wanted a bath. Dust and sand were in his hair, in and under all his clothes, chafing his skin and already forming into mud as his camp chores caused him to break into a sweat. His mouth was dry and gritty, but he put off taking a drink for just a little while longer. He would need the water much more as the day wore on.

The sheriff went over to the little mustang that the leader of the Comancheros had been riding and gave it the last of the water from the canteen that had been tied to the saddle. The other two horses had run off, and Horton wished that he had the water that they had taken with them. While he was there, he put Tommy Duncan's rig on the mustang, then he finished saddling the roan. Before the sun had cleared the horizon he was back on the trail, heading for Eagle Pass.

The sign of Duncan's passing had long since been blotted from the trail by the wind. Still, Horton kept a sharp watch. He was not alone in the land, as the events of the previous afternoon had reminded him. He took a little more time, stopping just short of the crest of each hill to check the land ahead of him. He saw no dust, no sign of a hard-running horse. He kept on, determined to find his man.

He knew that Duncan could be fifty yards off the trail in any direction, totally invisible and unlikely to be found by man, but somehow, he doubted that Duncan would lay in ambush for him. Oh, he'd fight if he was cornered, Horton believed, but he'd had plenty of opportunity to bushwhack him during the past week and had never tried. Horton's guess was that the kid would ride until he was caught, then all bets would be off. The kid knew that he'd hang in Benton, and he'd fight for his life to avoid that.

For the hundredth time Horton asked himself why he continued this chase. The kid had only held the horses. Back East some smart carpetbagging lawyer would probably be able to make a case that Duncan hadn't known what he was doing, that he'd only held the horses while his friends went into the bank to do some business. He'd say that once there they'd decided to try their hand at robbery and had failed miserably. The argument would end by suggesting to the jury that Duncan had run as soon as he saw what his friends were up to.

Horton thought that an argument like that just might work back east, but a Texas jury would want to see a hanging, whether or not Tommy Duncan had fired a shot or knew what his friends were up to. And Horton would follow him until he either caught him or died trying. It might be dumb, but it was still a matter of honor for the sheriff. And that sense of honor was more important to him than the kid, himself, or the woman he loved. Horton rode on.

It was nearly noon when the sheriff approached another low hill. There was nothing special about it; he'd crossed dozens just like it since he'd started that day. But the lawman sensed something. Some instinct told him to go slow.

Horton dismounted and tied the roan and the mustang to a cedar and started for the hill on foot. He'd taken only a step or two before he decided to leave his spurs behind, too. He took them off and hung them over his saddle horn, then moved up to the crest of the hill.

The last few yards Horton made on his belly, his Winchester cradled in his arms. Once at the top, he laid the rifle aside and used his binoculars to check the land ahead. He first scanned the left side of the trail and then the right. He saw nothing. He was about to shift his search to more distant parts of the trail when something caught his eye, and he snapped the binoculars back to the place where he thought he'd seen something.

It took Horton some time to finally decide what he had seen. There had been no movement, nothing to give away a man in ambush, but a man was there, nevertheless. There was a gentle mound under the mesquite by the side of the trail. It was about the length of a man. It might even have been a shallow grave. But Horton had seen the corner of a ground sheet that had not been covered by dirt. It was as though the concealing dirt had been dislodged when a man had crawled beneath it. Most men would never have seen the sheet and would not have thought twice about it if they had. But Horton was not like most men.

The sheriff inched back from the top of the hill and skirted around the rim to come out behind the mound.

He moved as silently as he could, wishing that there was a little wind to help cover the noise of his movement, but there was not a breath of wind to be found anywhere. Nevertheless, he moved on, slowly and very silently.

It took him an hour to come within easy pistol shot of the mound. Horton decided not to press his luck further. He dropped to one knee, aimed the Winchester dead center on the mound, and thumbed back the hammer.

"Come out from under the tarp with your hands up," the sheriff directed softly. "I got you in my sights."

Nothing happened.

Horton shifted his aim to a point just to the left and in front of the mound and squeezed the trigger. The rifle recoiled against his shoulder, and he levered another round into the chamber almost before the bullet struck the ground.

"Next time I aim for center mass," the lawman said.

There was movement under the mound and Tommy Duncan rolled slowly into view. He sat up slowly and raised his hands over his head.

"Didn't think I'd fool you," the kid said, "but I had to try."

"Gonna shoot me as I passed?" Horton asked.

"No, at least I don't think so," the kid answered honestly. "I was gonna help myself to your horse, though."

"What if it hadn't of been me?" Horton asked. "What would you of done then?"

"I 'spect I'd of taken the man's horse if I could an' I'd of been in big trouble if I couldn't, same as now," Tommy replied.

"Well, there's nothin' to be gained from 'what-ifin'. Get on your feet an' we'll walk back to the horses. I brung your gear with me."

Tommy's face lit up. "Did you say 'horses'? I was fearful that you'd make me walk back."

Horton kept the Winchester centered on the kid's belly.

"Before we get to be big pals again, you'd best un-buckle that gun belt and let it fall. And use your left hand to do it."

Duncan did as he had been told.

"An' while you're at it, take that pigsticker from outta the scabbard at the back of your neck an' add it to the pile," Horton added.

Tommy smiled and gently eased the Arkansas Toothpick from its hiding place and dropped it on the gun belt.

"Anything else you got stashed away?" the sheriff asked.

Tommy grinned sheepishly and brought out a .36 caliber Colt Model 1862 Police from the small of his back. He held it out in front of him with his thumb and index finger, then let it drop.

"Since I learned that trick from you, I thought I'd better fess up," the kid said.

Horton's expression remained grim. "Is that all or do I gotta strip you? Your word, now."

"Honest, Matt, that's the lot. I ain't never lied to you an' I ain't gonna start now."

"You ain't never been in this kind of trouble before, neither," Horton answered. "Step back into the center of the trail while I pick this stuff up."

"My Henry's under the tarp," Tommy said. "I'd hate for you to leave it behind. It's a good one."

Horton picked up the kid's weapons, then sent him back to collect his bedroll and canteen. While the outlaw got ready to travel, Horton asked him how he had collected the wound on his head. Tommy told him the story, at least as much as he could remember.

"So, you got your horse stole," It was a statement of fact, not a question. "How'd you like havin' what's yours taken by force?" the sheriff asked.

"Not worth a damn," the kid replied, "an' the horse wasn't even mine. It belonged to a young buck named Yellow Horse. I lived with him an' the rest of his family for years. He was my friend an' blood brother, an' then he tried to kill me. He thinks I killed his brother."

"Well, did you?" Horton asked.

"Hell, no!" the kid exploded. "I owed a lot to those people, even if I was somethin' of a prisoner. They could of killed me but they took me in instead. I owed 'em!"

"You don't have to convince me," Horton reminded the kid. "Start walkin' over the hill. We need to be gettin' on our way."

The two men walked back to the horses in silence.

Yellow Horse was in an evil mood. His father rode at the head of nearly a hundred warriors and he, his only son, rode in the back, choking on the dust thrown up by the horses.

The scene with his father in the camp the previous day had been bad enough. He could still feel the sting of humiliation as he relived those minutes in the tepee. It was the attitude of the tribe that hurt him most of all. They were treating him with sympathy or ignoring him altogether. They were not treating him as an equal, a Comanche warrior.

He had managed to acquire a horse, and he still had a bow and more than a dozen fine dogwood arrows, and he had his shield, made of hardened buffalo hide and adorned with many bear's teeth to show his prowess as a hunter. Clumps of hair from the tails of many horses hung on the shield to prove his success as a raider. After he had once collected scalps, they, too, would be displayed proudly on his shield. He prayed to the spirits that this would be the day when he would earn at least one such scalp on the field of battle.

At the front of the column, Spotted Calf stepped up the pace. The storm had wiped out all the tracks from yesterday, but he knew that Swift Eagle would head into the morning sun, toward the place the white man called Eagle Pass. Where else would anyone named Swift Eagle go? The spirits willed his passage.

As they continued along the trail, Spotted Calf discovered the fresh tracks that Horton had left that morning. Two horses, one rider, the Indian decided immediately after seeing the tracks. He could tell that neither horse was the one that his son had been riding just yesterday.

Then he corrected himself. Yellow Horse was no longer his son. The loss gave him great pain, more perhaps than the death of his son Running Buffalo. But he knew of no other way to force Yellow Horse to change his ways, to become a man instead of a spoiled child. He yearned for the day that he could be proud of Yellow Horse. He hoped that he lived long enough to see it.

Chapter 12

Jack and Harry had weathered the storm. In fact, by noon the following day Harry could focus his eyes and even eat without immediately heaving it back. Jack was a little disappointed with having to share their meager rations, but he, too, was doing some better. He still could not lower his arm past his waist, but the throbbing pain had lessened, and he hoped that soon the bones would begin to mend. The bandage on his hand had loosened considerably as the swelling had gone down, and that morning Harry had rewrapped it. The hand was still a frightful mass of purple and green and blue, but there was no open wound and no sign of infection. Jack knew that if nothing else happened, he would someday be able to use the hand again, but he suspected that he would never again be able to use it to hold a gun. That angered him beyond reason. Who ever heard of a gunman who couldn't handle a six-gun?

Jack kicked at a stump, felt the jar along his foot and leg, then swore.

"What's wrong, Jack?" Harry wanted to know.

"This place is what's wrong. The food's bad, the company ain't much better, an' there's nuthin' to drink. It's time for us to go back to that tradin' post."

"I don't know, Jack," Harry said. "We got enough to get by for another day, an' if there's anyone left around there after the storm to help the Mex, we could be in a lot of trouble. I think we ought to wait another day."

Jack cast him an evil glance. "Since when did you start doin' the thinkin' for this gang, anyway? I say that it's the time to teach that Mex a lesson, an' we're gonna do it now. Saddle the horses an' we'll ride."

Harry got to his feet and began saddling the horses.

"We ain't much of a gang, Jack," the outlaw said. "It's just me 'n you. I got a say in this, just as much as you." But he said it low, where there would be no chance that Jack would overhear.

"Quit mumblin' an' get busy!" Jack yelled.

Harry did his best.

Pedro O'Brien bent over to pick up a pail and staggered. As he straightened, he uttered a groan and repressed an urge to vomit. He had finished a bottle of Irish whiskey during the storm, and now he was paying the penalty for his evening of debauchery.

Bucket in hand, Pedro opened the back door and recoiled in pain. The sunlight was intense, turning his brain into a cauldron of molten fire. Never in his forty years had he experienced such pain. He staggered through the door, but he only made a couple of paces before the pain in his head and his turbulent stomach finally connected. He fell to his hands and knees and retched until nothing else would come up. Finally, he made it back to his feet. The bucket lay on its side on the ground.

"To hell with it," Pedro said aloud. "The horses will have to be patient a little while longer. I cannot stand the light another moment." He narrowed his eyes to slits and stepped back into the cool darkness of his trading post, closing the door gently behind him.

Pedro walked over to his cot and looked down in disgust at the bottle that lay near the pillow. He picked it up and flung it into the corner, sorry even before it broke about the unnecessary noise he had created. He collapsed with a moan onto the rumpled blankets and threw an arm across his eyes.

"Never again," he promised himself. "Never again."

But in his heart Pedro knew that the next time he was alone and there was a storm, he would seek comfort from a bottle. Soon he was snoring loudly.

It took Jack and Harry nearly two hours to ride to Cedar Station. They went slow to keep from jarring Jack's hand any more than necessary. The two men reigned to a halt about three hundred yards from the station just inside a stand of mesquite. They watched as Pedro emerged into the yard for the second time that day. This time the station keeper was successful in watering and caring for the stock in the stable. The horses in the stone corral had plenty of water in the trough, so Pedro forked in some hay and went back into the trading post.

The horsemen sat and watched for several minutes. They saw no one else, and no strange horses were anywhere to be seen.

"I think the Mex is alone," Jack said as he smiled nastily. "Now's a good time to take him, before anyone else comes along to get in our way."

"How're we gonna do it?" Harry wanted to know. "We got no guns or nuthin'."

Jack looked at the other man as if he were an idiot and then explained his plan.

"I'm gonna get in the corral and get those horses all mad," he said. "You're gonna get a piece of that stove wood offa the pile an' stand by the back door, When the Mex comes out to see what's happenin' to the horses, you bash his brains out."

Harry thought about it for a while, but he could find no flaw in the plan. He really didn't want to do this but faced with a choice between angering Jack or bashing the proprietor, he guessed that it would be easier and safer to bash O'Brien.

The two men dismounted and tied their horses in the brush. They could see no doors or window shutters open, but they moved up to the station carefully anyway. Jack slipped into the corral and Harry selected a two-foot length of stove wood before positioning himself against the wall next to the back door. When they were both set, Harry took off his hat and waved it violently as he let out a squall that would have shattered glass.

And nothing happened. Jack whooped and hollered, the horses screamed in fright and ran around in panic, and the back door of the trading post remained shut. Then, finally, as Jack was about to drop from exhaustion, the door opened and Pedro stepped outside.

"What's wrong with you crazy animals?" he said as he took an unsteady step towards the corral.

Just then he saw movement out of the corner of his eye. He started to turn and to throw up an arm to protect himself, but he was too late. The piece of stove wood striking Pedro's head made a sound like an ax burying itself in a stump. Pedro's knees collapsed and he fell into a heap in the dust.

"Hit him again! Jack shouted in glee from the corral.

"Do I gotta? The other man replied. "Shouldn't we keep him alive in case he's hid his money or somethin'?"

While Jack was not exactly overjoyed to hear his inferior voice an opinion or make a suggestion, he had to admit that Harry's question had merit. The Mexican might just prove to be more useful to them alive than dead.

"Don't let it go to your head, Harry, but you might just be right. Drag him inside an' tie him up tight while I see if he's got anything we can use."

When Harry tried to drag the heavy man inside, he began to have second thoughts about saving the station owner. He grunted and strained and finally got O'Brien onto his cot. After taking a minute to catch his breath, he found some rope and tied the man's hands and feet securely. Then he looked around for Jack.

The other outlaw was behind the bar, chuckling happily. He had a beer in his fist and the cash box opened on the bar. He took a drink, wiped his mouth on his sleeve, and set the beer down on the bar.

"There must be fifty to sixty dollars in here!" he shouted. "An' our guns are here under the bar!"

Jack brought the guns out, one at a time. He checked his own before sliding them into their holsters, then watched as Harry did the same. The weight of the weapons felt good on Jack's hips, and suddenly his hand didn't hurt as much.

"See what's in the pot on the stove," Jack commanded and then turned back to the money as his partner inspected the contents.

"Looks like some kind o' stew," Harry reported. He stuck his finger in the stew and then into his mouth. "Don't taste bad, neither. You want that I should heat it up?"

Jack looked at him in that special way again, so Harry built up a fire and positioned the pot over it.

Soon the aroma of food wafted through the room. Jack tore himself away from the bar long enough to find a couple of plates and some spoons, which he deposited on a table. When the stew was hot, Harry ladled a batch of it onto each plate, then brought over a loaf of bread and a knife. The men ate in silence until the plates were clean. Harry filled them again and they ate until they could hold no more.

Jack belched with such force that the bottles behind the bar must have rattled.

"I'll say this for the Mex. He sure knows how to make a stew," he said. "Wonder what he puts in it?"

"You don't want to know," Harry said. He'd had more than a little experience with border cooking. "Just eat it an' enjoy. What you don't know about won't make you sick."

Jack laughed. He was definitely feeling better. He leaned back in his chair and surveyed the room. In his greed he looked for ways to take everything that was in the station, but in the end, practicality dictated that they take only what they could comfortably carry on their horses.

"Start gettin' a pack made up with food, clothes, ammunition, an' some whiskey," he said to Harry. "As soon as he wakes up, we'll find out if he's got any more money around here."

Jack slowly got up and went over to inspect the unconscious O'Brien. "Wish you hadn't hit him so damn hard. He may be out for hours."

Harry shrugged in apology and set about making up a pack. Jack went to the bar and drank another beer before pocketing the money. He thought that it was quite likely that Harry would forget all about the cash as long as he didn't see any of it laying around. Jack laughed. There were benefits to having a stupid partner, he thought.

Harry watched Jack slip the money into his pocket and he knew that the other man meant to cheat him, He filed the information away for use later. Harry would give Jack anything he asked for, but he wouldn't be cheated. Not in this life.

Chapter 13

Horton topped a small rise and looked behind him. There was dust in the distance—lots of it. He motioned for Duncan to pull up and dismount. The sheriff swung down from the roan, took the binoculars from his saddlebags, and studied the dust. The riders, whoever they were, were too far away for the lawman to see. Still, even that told him something. There had to be a lot of riders back there to make that much dust.

Tommy walked over to Horton and borrowed the lawman's glasses. He, too, scanned their backtrail.

"Any idea who they are?" Horton asked.

"Can't tell any more'n you, but if I had to make a wager, my money'd be on Yellow Horse an' his friends. A lot of his friends, it looks like." Duncan handed the binoculars back to the sheriff and walked back over to his horse.

"That's what I thought, too," Horton admitted. "You seem to be hotter'n a two-bit pistol. Is there anybody else after you that I ought to know about? You ain't managed to get the Mescalero Apache mad at you, too, have you?"

Duncan raised his canteen to his mouth, took a swallow, then lowered the canteen. He tamped the cork stopper back in the neck and then turned back to the sheriff.

"Matt, as far as I know I got problems with you and the Comanche, an' one of those is a bum deal. That dust back there may not be Yellow Horse, but if it is, he's got every damn warrior in the tribe with him. I think we got one choice. We can run like hell back to Cedar Station an' try to make a stand there. We're dead meat if they catch us out here."

Horton pushed his hat back on his head and wiped the sweat from his brow. He poured a little of his water on his bandana and wiped out the nostrils of his horse, then tucked the bandana in his belt. It would be dry again in a few minutes.

"You may be right," the lawman said. "We'll head east from here an' see if they follow. If they do, we'll cut north again an' make a run for it."

"How about given' my guns back to me?" Tommy asked. "If that is Yellow Horse, you're gonna need all the help you can get."

"If it is Yellow Horse, I'll give 'em back to you in trade for your word that you won't use 'em to escape. 'Til then, I'll just keep 'em so you don't get too tempted."

Duncan started to protest but saw the strain and the grim look of determination etched on the older man's face.

"I'm sorry I got you into this, Matt," he said softly. "I was a damn fool."

"If you're lookin' for an argument from me, you're gonna be disappointed. Now get back aboard that mustang. We can't afford to lose any more time."

The two men remounted and turned east as soon as they came to a patch of rocky ground that might cover their tracks. The ruse might work or it might not. The only thing that was sure was that they had to try.

Spotted Calf came upon the bodies of the dead Comancheros. They checked the bodies only to see if one of them was that of Swift Eagle or if they had any ammunition on them. Once they were satisfied that nothing useful was to be found, the war party rode on, following the trail that Horton had left. They did not linger at the site of the lawman's capture of Duncan, either, but they did turn north to follow the trail that the two men had left.

Spotted Calf did not like the amount of dust they were creating, but there was little that they could do about it. It was not possible for a war party this big to remain hidden from sight. They must trade stealth for speed, find their enemies, and overwhelm them swiftly. The second man, the one who had caught Swift Eagle, would be killed quickly, but the man who had killed his son would die as slowly as he could make it happen. He remembered one man, a hunter who had raped a woman in the tribe. It had taken him four suns to die. Perhaps Swift Eagle would take five.

Yellow Horse had moved up in the column. From time to time, he would leave it entirely, moving a considerable distance to the east of the others, partly because he hoped to get out of the dust and partly because he hoped to beat the others in the attack when they finally overtook Swift Eagle and the other man. No one seemed to care what he did. It was as if he were not even there.

Yellow Horse continued to brood. He longed for his father to yell at him, hit him, even. Being ignored was the worst imaginable humiliation. No one would dare to talk to him until his father did. For that to happen, he knew that he must redeem himself in the eyes of his father.

Hour after hour the column moved on. The speed of the war party was taking a toll on the horses, and the column was getting strung out. Most of the warriors had brought along an extra horse, and they were the ones who ended up near the head of the column. Yellow Horse had no extra animal. Periodically, he would slide from his horse's back and run alongside. The horse, relieved of the man's weight, was rested in that way. Yellow Horse did not tire. Hatred and anger kept him going, wiping everything from his mind except the thought of killing Swift Eagle and regaining the favor of his father.

It was late afternoon when Yellow Horse, riding a far rifle shot to the east of the war party, saw the dim outline of tracks headed due east. He pulled his horse brutally to a stop and slid to the ground. His heart leaped in his breast. These were the tracks of two men, moving quickly. He recognized the tracks of the big roan from the day before.

Had it only been the day before? he mused. It seemed like a lifetime. He remounted his horse and let out a whoop as he waved his shield back and forth over his head. He saw the column stop and he kicked his pony in the sides to hurry it as he rode to find his father.

Yellow Horse pulled his mount to a stop beside Spotted Calf. He held his excitement within himself and tried with some success to appear calm.

"Honored One," he said, not yet willing to risk the wrath of Spotted Calf by calling him father, "I have found the tracks of Swift Eagle and his companion. They have turned," he said as he pointed east. "They are riding swiftly and staying on rocky ground."

Spotted Calf said nothing but signaled for two of the closest braves to go where Yellow Horse had indicated to see for themselves. While they were gone, no one said a word. The only sounds to be heard were those made by the horses.

Within minutes the braves returned, verifying what Yellow Horse had reported. Spotted Calf moved his horse close to his son's. He reached out and clasped him on the shoulder. Yellow Horse resisted the urge to flinch from his father's touch.

"My son," Spotted Calf said with some emotion, "you have done well. But for your sure eye we might have lost the trail of Swift Eagle. Come, ride beside me, that if he turns again before we sight him you will not let him escape from us."

Yellow Horse could hardly believe his ears. His father had called him his son, and he had been granted the position of honor at his side.

The young warrior straightened his back and sat a little taller. Gone now was any trace of fatigue that he might have felt. He threw out his chest in pride.

"I am honored, father," he responded. "I hope to be worthy of your confidence."

A flicker of a smile crossed Spotted Calf's face and then he urged his horse forward again, following the trail that his son had pointed out. The rest of the war party followed.

As they rode, Yellow Horse thought of how wise he had been to ride apart from the rest. His father and even the great trackers had missed the spot where Swift Eagle had turned, but he alone had saved them from hours of wasted searching. Swift Eagle might have gotten away altogether had it not been for his keen eyes and his skill in reading sign. And so, he dreamed as he rode along next to his father.

Spotted Calf smiled to himself. He had wondered if his son would spot the tracks which they now followed. He had slowed the other warriors so that Yellow Horse might have the time he needed to see the tracks, and he had prayed to the Great One that his son would see what any blind man could see instantly. He did not know what he would have done if Yellow Horse had missed the sign. He was glad that he had not needed to find out.

Tommy Duncan looked over his shoulder again. The sun was beginning to set, and the bright rays made clear vision difficult to the west, but there was no mistaking the fact that the dust cloud had shifted. The war party had found the point where they had turned and had turned with them.

The young man turned to speak to Horton, but the lawman spoke first.

"Yeah, I know. We didn't fool 'em none. Probably foolish to think we might. There's a creek up ahead about a mile or two. We'll follow it north as far as we can. Maybe the water'll wipe out our tracks."

"How about my guns, Matt?" Tommy asked. "There can't be any question now about who's followin' us."

"Later," the sheriff said. "You don't need 'em yet."

Light was nearly gone when the two men came upon the stream. It was only a few inches deep and the water did not flow very fast. Tracks would take a long time to wash away under these conditions.

The two men dismounted and let their horses drink as they filled their canteens upstream. They took a few minutes to strip off most of their clothes and wash some of the accumulated dirt from their bodies. They shook out their pants and put them back on and rinsed their shirts and tied them to their bedrolls. Then they mounted up and headed north, staying in the streambed.

Horton decided that they would ride as long as they could before making a cold camp for the evening. He doubted that the Comanche would follow once the sun set completely, but he wasn't sure. No one could ever be sure about anything where the Comanche were concerned.

The two men rode in the stream for about an hour before it suddenly veered east and stayed flowing in that direction. Horton found a rocky spot on the bank and turned south, then halted about a hundred yards into the brush. The two men dismounted and tied their horses, then broke off mesquite branches and went back to the stream, sweeping out their tracks as they walked back to their horses.

Once back at the horses they unsaddled the animals and made camp. Horton picked up Duncan's weapons and walked over to him.

"You'll take the first watch tonight," he said. "Wake me about midnight an' I'll take over. You'll need these," he said as he handed Tommy the weapons. "Just in case you see somethin'."

"You've got my word that I won't try to escape as long as we got Indian problems," the young man promised as he checked his weapons. "I won't pull no sneak stuff on you."

"If I thought you would, you'd be hogtied right now," the sheriff answered. "Now shut up so I can sleep."

Duncan smiled in the dark. Horton could hear an ant breathe, and he knew it. The sheriff might have been rolled up in his blanket, but in his hand he held a Colt, and the Winchester was within easy reach, too. Tommy took his Henry and found a good place from which to keep watch. He put on his shirt, but he left his blanket behind. A little cold would help him to stay alert. It might also help keep him alive.

Spotted Calf held up his hand as a signal for the war party to halt. It was dark now, and sign was too hard to follow. The bank of Comanche had gotten as far as the creek, and Spotted Calf decided that this would be a good place to stop for the night. He motioned for Yellow Horse to come nearer.

"My son, take a warrior with you and discover which way Swift Eagle went from here. I think that very soon he must turn again. He may have followed this water or continued on a little farther. Find out what he has done and come back to tell me."

"Yes, father," Yellow Horse said obediently. He wanted to continue on, to run Swift Eagle to ground, but he knew that this was not the time to challenge the authority of his father.

Yellow Horse selected the best tracker in the tribe after himself and moved away from the Comanche camp. There were no tracks to be seen east of the creek, so the pair dismounted and walked into the water in search of sign, which they quickly found. Hoof prints take a long time to fill in if the water was shallow or not very swift. This creek was both. The men left the water and led their mounts back to the camp. Yellow Horse quickly sought out Spotted Calf.

"Swift Eagle has used the water to head that way," he said, pointing to the north. "We did not follow the track very far. Shall we go back and continue after him?"

"You have done well to find the track," the old one said. "We will wait until morning to follow. The water may seep away that sign, but it cannot sweep the ground where they leave the water. We will find that sign tomorrow."

The old man was silent for a while, then turned to his son and said, "Where do they go? Think of the ground and what they may choose between. You know the way of the white man. Tell me where they are headed."

Yellow Horse thought for several minutes. White men sought out other white men when they were in trouble. They liked towns first, and high ground where they could shoot down on those who attacked them. They carried with them much food because they could not live well off the land. Yellow Horse considered all of these things before he spoke.

"I believe, my father, that they will go to the trading post," he finally said.

"Why did you pick that place?" his father asked.

Yellow Horse explained his reasoning. "Also, they will have much food and water and ammunition there," he added.

"You have considered well," the old man said. "Of course you are right. In the morning you will take twenty warriors and ride swiftly to the trading post. Burn it and then wait. I will bring the others, and we will drive the white men before us into the slaughter."

Yellow Horse nodded his head in acknowledgment. He did not trust himself to speak. He was filled with pride that he had thought correctly and that his father had entrusted him with a special task.

Tomorrow Swift Eagle would die, and he would be the one who killed him.

Chapter 14

It was closer to three than it was to midnight when Tommy finally woke Horton to stand watch. He had correctly assumed that the sheriff would spend the first hour or more watching him to make sure that he wouldn't run off. The young outlaw felt guilty about Matt's being out there anyway, so he let him sleep until he found his own eyes getting heavy.

The sheriff rolled out of his blanket, pistol in hand, when Duncan was still a dozen feet away.

"Midnight?" the older man asked as he rubbed the sleep from his eyes.

"Some later than that," Tommy replied. "I wasn't tired an' you looked like you was enjoyin' your sleep, so I left you be. I'm tired now, though."

Horton tipped his boots upside down and shook them just in case a scorpion had decided to take a nap there. Finding no unwanted visitors, he slipped his feet into the boots, picked up his Winchester, his shirt, and his blanket, and walked into the brush. Duncan found his blanket and rolled up in it, not bothering to undress. If there was going to be any trouble, he wouldn't have time to get dressed anyway.

It seemed as though he had just closed his eyes when he felt Horton nudging him awake.

"Come on, boy, the day's half over," the lawman said gently.

The younger man sat up and looked around. The sun was just beginning to glow red below the eastern horizon, and it was still too black to see more than a few feet in any direction. He stood up and looked around for his saddle.

"I got the horses ready while you was sleepin'," the lawman said. "You don't sleep much, but you damn sure sleep hard. How'd you manage to stay alive all these years?"

Tommy smiled, knowing that his leg was being pulled. "I don't waste a bunch of good sleepin' time tryin' to watch the watcher. Man's gotta be able to trust somebody, an' who better to trust than the law?"

Horton snorted in reply as he walked over to the horses. He mounted and waited for the younger man to relieve himself and then mount and get settled in his saddle.

"We're goin' due north from here. We'll cut the stream about two hundred yards past where we came out, but we'll sweep out our tracks on both banks. After that we'll ride like hell for the trading post," the lawman directed.

"Good plan, Matt. They know where we are an' where we're goin'. I'd bet on it."

"Let's go, then, before those friends of yours drop by for breakfast," Matt said.

They rode off into the brush together.

Dawn found Pedro O'Brien straining at his ropes in a desperate attempt to get loose. The station was dark, the windows shuttered and barred. His unwelcome guests were asleep near the doors, but the proprietor knew that sooner or later they would awaken and if he was still there, he'd be in for a rough time.

His head still hurt, but nothing was broken. He'd taken inventory as best he could as soon as he had regained consciousness. He had no feeling in his hands, and he had soiled himself sometime during the night, but he guessed that mostly what had been damaged was his dignity, at least so far.

Pedro squirmed around but all he succeeded in doing was to make the sleepers restless. He decided that his best bet shot of escape was to postpone the time of their awakening for as long as possible. To that end he lay still, hoping against hope that someone would come to rescue him before the two gunmen awoke.

It was nearly noon when Jack finally decided to open his eyes. He'd drunk a lot the night before, and his bladder was near to bursting. He rolled out of his cot and made his way outside to the privy. It was some time before he returned, fully awake and much refreshed. He walked over and kicked the soles of Harry's boots.

"C'mon, Harry, it's time to get up, We gotta leave here pretty soon."

Harry groaned and then sat up and swung his boots to the floor. He rubbed his eyes with both fists, then put on his hat and made a trip outside for the same purpose that Jack had a few minutes earlier.

When he returned, Jack and Harry went over to check on Pedro, who lay still with his eyes closed.

"You reckon I killed him?" Harry asked.

"I doubt it," the outlaw answered. "I got a feeling that the Mex is playin' possum. Stoke up that fire an' stick an iron in it. We'll toast his toes an' see if he's still sleepy."

Pedro's eyes sprang open in terror.

"Now lookie there, he's awake after all," Jack observed. "He's had a remarkable recovery, don't you think?"

"Whatever you say, Jack. What are we gonna do with him now?"

"First you do what I said," Jack replied. "I got a real good response from him when I started talkin' about usin' a hot iron on him. Maybe he's got somethin' that he really wants to tell us. We got time to listen while the iron's gettin' hot."

Pedro's eyes got very large. "Tell me what you want. If I've got it, it's yours. You need not trouble yourselves with the iron. Nothing I've got is worth that much."

"Now you're talkin' sense, Mex," Jack said, "but we'll heat the iron just in case you get forgetful." He turned and looked at Harry.

"Just don't stand there. Get busy an' do what I tol' you."

Harry stoked up the fire in the stove and stuck a poker into the fire box. Then he walked back over to Jack and the proprietor.

"Now, Mex, tell us where all your money's hid," Jack said.

"It's in the cashbox behind the bar," Pedro replied immediately.

"I mean the rest of it," Jack said as he grabbed a fist full of the man's shirt and hauled him into a sitting position.

Pedro swung his feet to the floor in order to keep his balance and then said with all the conviction he would muster. "That's all the money I got here. My wife an' my hired man went off to buy more supplies. You can see for yourself that the shelves are almost empty. That's the truth—I swear it."

Jack backhanded Pedro and then he drew his pistol.

"I don't shoot so good lefthanded, my friend, but I shoot good enough so's I can kill you. Now tell me the truth. Where's the rest of the money?" Jack thumbed back the hammer as if to emphasize his question.

"I've told you the truth, señor! I have no more money besides what's in the cashbox. If I had more, I'd give it to you gladly. But even I cannot make money appear when there is none."

Jack aimed his pistol at a spot between Pedro's eyes and began taking up the slack in the trigger. He watched in amusement as the proprietor began to sweat profusely.

"Please, señor, I have told you the truth. Do not kill me," Pedro begged.

Harry reached over and shoved Jack's pistol aside just as he fired. The slug buried itself somewhere in a pile of blankets.

Jack swung towards his partner, anger flashing in his eyes.

"What'd you do that for?" he demanded.

"He told you what you wanted to know," Harry answered, "an' you got all his money in your pocket. We ain't gonna kill him, Jack, not just so you can watch him die. We can fight about it if you want, but you ain't real fast lefthanded, an' you ain't up to no fist fight. I think maybe you'd better back off an' behave yourself. You can begin by puttin' your gun away. You ain't gonna use it."

Harry had just possibly made the longest speech of his young life. It was certainly the only time when he had ever stood up against anybody, and he liked the feeling.

Jack, however, was not so happy about this turn of events. He thought of drawing against Harry, but suddenly he doubted that he would be fast enough. He thought that it was quite possible that Harry would kill him. He felt a touch of fear and decided that it was time for this partnership to break up, one way or another. When they rode away from here, Jack was determined that they'd ride their separate ways. That is, unless Harry turned his back before then. In that case, only Jack would ride away.

Yellow Horse and his band were riding hard within minutes of the time Horton and Duncan broke camp. They rose along parallel paths but were separated by four or five miles of brush-choked terrain. Slowly the war party drew ahead of Horton and Duncan, for they rode with no concern for their horses. Yellow Horse was interested only in making it to the trading post before Swift Eagle. His father expected it and he vowed that he would not fail him.

Horton saw the dust to the west of them after the sun had risen fully. He also saw the dust to their rear and knew that their attempts to hide their tracks had proved to be useless. He feared that the Comanche knew where they were headed and would beat them there. He shared his thoughts with Duncan.

"I've thought so all along," the young man replied. "An' we can't go any faster. These horses are a long way from bein' fresh an' we're askin' 'em to carry about fifty pounds more'n those mustangs carry. We may end up havin' to shoot our way into the station yet."

The two men rode on, watching the dust cloud to the west pull steadily ahead of them. But what really worried the two was the dust cloud behind them. The war party that made it was getting closer, too, although not as rapidly as the other war party was drawing away from them. Before long they would be boxed, and there was no way for them to avoid it. They could only keep on going, moving ever closer to their fate, whatever that might be, and trust in luck. And luck, it would seem, had taken a holiday.

Chapter 15

Pedro O'Brien was in agony. Harry had cut him loose, and blood flowed back into his hands for the first time in hours. He had experienced pain before, but nothing to match this. He wished that he could get to the bottle of Irish whiskey behind the bar, but he didn't want to get that far away from Harry. He also did not want to give Jack any ideas. That man was strange enough sober; drunk he would be a madman. Pedro still remembered the fight that had taken place right there in that room only three days before, although it seemed like a lifetime ago. And if Jack ever found out who had crushed his hand, Pedro knew he would be a dead man, Harry or no Harry.

As the circulation was restored to Pedro's hands, the pain eased into a persistent throbbing. After a while he could flex his fingers again and, although they still looked as if they had been scalded, Pedro decided that he could use them sufficiently well to get himself cleaned up. After some discussion between Jack and Harry, none of it very friendly, Pedro was allowed to change clothing. After that he was put to work cooking breakfast. Soon coffee was boiling and the fragrant aroma of frying bacon and beans bubbling in the pot filled the station. The world seemed a little brighter, and even Jack's foul mood seemed to improve a bit.

Harry kept a close eye on Jack and was particularly careful not to turn his back on him. Pedro was gaining new respect and appreciation for Harry's good sense.

When the food was ready, Pedro dished up a batch of stuff on a metal plate and delivered it to Jack, who took it sullenly to a counter and began eating. The proprietor fixed a similar plate for Harry.

"Why'd you do it, Harry? Why'd you keep Jack from killin' me?" he asked softly.

"I don't know," the man answered. "I guess I just got a good look at Jack an' me, an' I didn't much care for what I saw. I thought Jack was really somethin', you know, an' the—well, it's like he ain't nuthin' but trash. My pa talked again' folks like him, but I thought he must be pretty dumb, bein' over fifty an' all, with nuthin' but forty acres of bottom land and a shack with walls what had cracks so big you would throw a cat through 'em without touchin' a board. That, headaches an' blisters was all that ol' man had to show for his whole life. I wanted more, but if I stick with Jack, I'll never see thirty, let alone fifty, an' all I'll have to show for it is a length of new rope."

Harry snorted. "Listen to me, will ya? I ain't said that much at one time in ten years."

Pedro smiled and patted the man on the shoulder. "I think you're wrong about your father," he said. "He's got a pretty damn good son to show for his life. That's about as good as anybody's got a right to expect."

Harry blushed from his neck to the roots of his hair. He started to say something and then thought better of it. A minute or so later he said simply, "Thanks."

While the men were eating, Pedro helped himself to a plate full of beans and some bacon. He ate quickly, then refilled the plates of the others.

"Harry," he said in a loud voice, "I need to take care of the horses. Is that all right with you?"

"Yeah, go ahead," Harry said.

"Hell, no, it ain't all right!" Jack exploded.

"But señor, the horses must be cared for if you plan to have anything to ride when you leave here," Pedro reasoned.

"An' you probably got a gun or a machete or somethin' else hidden out there in the barn," Jack said. "You stay in here. We ain't goin' nowhere anyway."

"Pedro, go take care of the horses," Harry said. "If you come in here with a gun or somethin', I'll kill you myself. Go do your chores."

Pedro slipped out the door and shut it firmly behind him.

Jack exploded. "He'll get a gun or ride out o' here! How could you be so damn stupid?"

Harry said softly, "So what? If he comes in with a gun, he's dead. If he leaves, it'll be days before he can get anywhere an' then come back. We'll be long gone by then, an' you already got all his money. What're you afraid of anyway, Jack?"

"I ain't afraid of that damn Mex, that's for sure. I just don't like you makin' all the decisions around here. You ain't very smart."

"Get used to it, Jack," the other man said. "I'm makin' the decisions for both of us 'til we leave. If you can't live with that, then stand up an' make your play. I don't care which it is, as long as it's settled right now."

Jack dearly wanted to draw his Colt, but he didn't have the nerve. He stewed about it for a while, then sat back in his chair.

"You got the better of me 'cause of my hand," he said sullenly, "but when we leave here, I'm given' the orders again, an' you get that straight in that thick head of yours."

"You'll be givin' orders to yourself, Jack. When we leave here, we're takin' different trails. I've had quite enough of you an' your temper an' your insults.

Jack couldn't believe his ears. He was speechless. This was unthinkable—mutiny, in fact.

Pedro came back into the room and slammed the door behind him. He spun on his heel, grabbed a plank, and barred the door. Then he turned to face the two startled men.

"Gentlemen," he said calmly, "we've got visitors."

Yellow Horse and his war party stopped their horses at the edge of the growth of mesquite and looked at the station some three hundred yards away. The ground had been cleared of all brush and other growth to that distance all the way around the station to prevent sneak attacks and to offer clear fields of fire for the defenders.

The warriors saw Pedro emerge from the building and go to the barn. They watched him come back out a few minutes later with feed for the horses in the stone corral. One of the horses there nickered in anticipation of being fed and one of the warrior's horses nickered back before its rider could silence him. They watched as the station owner froze in his tracks.

"It is time to take the station, my brothers!" Yellow Horse shouted to the others. He jabbed his heels into his horse's ribs and the animal leaped into the open, closely followed by twenty other mounted warriors.

Yellow Horse notched an arrow in his bow and let it fly in the direction of Pedro as soon as he came within range. By that time the station keeper had dropped the feed and was running for all he was worth for the station. The arrow missed him by inches, as did the next two or three that were released. Then the man was at the door and through it. An arrow thudded into the center of the door as it slammed shut.

The battle for Cedar Station had begun.

Horton and Duncan rode as hard as they dared, but the war party behind them gained ground rapidly. It was not long before riders became visible in the dust and then began to close the distance more quickly.

Horton and Duncan lost concern for the welfare of the horses they rode as they tried desperately to reach Cedar Station. They spurred their horses to greater efforts, but they still had more than three miles to go when Duncan's horse stepped into a hole and threw itself and its rider to the ground. The sound of the horse's leg breaking was like a gunshot.

Horton looked back and saw Tommy get unsteadily to his feet. The sheriff pulled up his horse and turned back toward the dismounted man. Tommy ran over to his horse, drew his pistol, and shot it in the head. Then he pulled the Henry from its scabbard and knelt behind the carcass. He began firing steadily at the rapidly approaching Indians.

"Get the hell out of here!" Duncan shouted to Horton. "I'll hold them off the best I can!"

Horton reined his horse to a stop and leaped to the ground, taking his Winchester with him. He pulled his horse's neck around, grabbed a forefoot, and threw the animal to the ground. The horse lay there quivering as the lawman knelt on his neck and began firing at the Comanche.

"Get out of here, Matt!" Tommy repeated. "There ain't no use both of us dyin' here. Get your horse up an' light out o' here!"

"Save your breath, son," the sheriff answered. "We'll leave together or we won't leave at all. You take the right side; I'll take the left. When they stop and pull back, we'll light out again. Now, start shootin'!"

The two men fired as fast as they could lever fresh cartridges into the chambers of their rifles. Three or four Comanches fell from their horses and two or three more slumped as if they had been hit. The Indians stopped their attack and rode back out of rifle range. The few warriors with rifles began firing, but the two men could not hear the passage of bullets.

Horton stood up, releasing his hold on the horse. The animal scrambled to its feet and Horton sprang into the saddle. He took his foot out of the stirrup, held out his hand, and yelled out to Tommy.

"Now, boy! Time's a wastin'!"

Duncan got to his feet and ran to Horton. Moments later the two men were riding the big roan towards Cedar Station as fast as the animal could go.

It did not take the Comanche long to follow the two men. The brief fight had caught them unprepared. They had a plan, but the fall of one rider had not been expected. By the time they had decided what to do, they had three dead braves and four others that were wounded too badly to ride. These men they left to fend for themselves the best they could. The war party was too close to stop for its wounded. It would not stop for anything or anyone until Swift Eagle was dead. Each warrior had given his word to Spotted Calf willingly, and now, with dead and wounded friends left behind, their resolve became even stronger. The white men would die that day, and if possible, they would die slowly and painfully.

The warriors rode swiftly after their quarry. They wanted this chase ended before the sun set for the day.

Jack and Harry ran to the shuttered windows and peered out through the firing ports. They ducked their heads aside as arrows and a few bullets thudded into the thick wood. Both men drew their pistols and began firing.

Pedro ran to the rifle rack and pulled down a Winchester and a 10-gauge shotgun. He grabbed a couple of boxes of shells for each off the shelves behind the counter and went to one of the windows on the opposite side of the station from the two men. He propped the rifle against the wall, dropped the cartridges for it alongside it on the floor, and began firing the shotgun methodically through the firing port.

Harry and Jack turned to look at the source of the noise, then turned back to their windows. Whatever arguments had been between men, all was forgotten now, or at least until after this fight was over. The three men were now united against a common enemy.

Shots continued to ring out, and brave men died. The war party had few rifles, and the defenders had thick walls to protect them. So far, the dying had been confined to the attackers, but everyone knew that the situation could change at any moment.

Chapter 16

Horton heard firing up ahead. They were within a mile of Cedar Station, but just then it looked like a hundred. The big roan was tired and seemed to be slowing with every step. The lawman was not sure that the animal could travel that last mile at a walk, let alone a run.

There was a gentle rise in front of them. The roan made it to the top but stumbled as he started down the other side. Horton reined him to a stop and both he and Duncan slipped to the ground. This time Horton did not throw the roan to the ground. The crest of the hill would protect the animal from the Comanche's fire. The two men ran back to the crest of the hill and threw themselves flat on the ground. They were just in time. Only moments later the war party rode into sight.

Horton fired first and saw his shot strike a warrior nearly two hundred yards away. As he levered a fresh round into the chamber of his Winchester, he quickly shifted his sights to a closer Comanche. He held his breath, squeezed the trigger, and felt the recoil against his shoulder as the rifle fired. Another warrior was flung from his horse into the brush.

Horton heard Duncan's Henry thunder as the kid fired steadily into the advancing Comanches, but he had little time to spare for him. He was too busy with the Indians before him. He fired as fast as he could, but this time the Indians did not stop or pull back. They kept on coming.

The lawman laid his sights on a warrior a scant fifty yards in front of him and squeezed the trigger. The hammer fell, striking the firing pin, but nothing happened. Horton worked the lever and tried again, with the same results. The rifle was empty, and there was no time to reload.

The sheriff dropped the rifle, drew his Colt, and fired, his bullet striking the warrior in the chest. The man threw up his arms and fell from his horse, his momentum carrying him forward until he struck the dirt not five yards in front of the lawman. Horton fired twice more without taking the time to see where his shots went, and then he was being crushed to the ground beneath the weight of a Comanche warrior.

The breath was nearly driven from Horton's body as he struck the ground. He rolled with his attacker, losing his grip on his Colt as he fought. Each man struggled to gain an advantage over the other. Horton heard the kid still firing steadily, but the significance of that was lost to him as he fought for his life against his determined adversary.

Horton smelled the Indian as they fought, a combination of sweat and dust and horse. The man fought well, gouging and punching whenever Horton presented an opening. Finally, the lawman was able to smash his forehead into the warrior's nose, breaking it. The big man grunted in pain, and he drew back just for a moment, giving Horton the chance to knee him viciously in the groin.

The blow was not enough to stop the warrior for good, but it was enough to allow Horton to break his opponent's grip, roll out from under him, and struggle to his feet. The Indian scrambled to his feet, too, and stood facing Horton, hatred blazing fiercely in his black eyes as blood streamed from his shattered nose.

The Comanche swiftly drew a knife from his belt and launched himself at the lawman. Horton sidestepped and swung a vicious right that struck the Indian on the ear. The man hit the ground but was up and quickly shaking his head to clear it as he circled his prey.

Horton feinted with a left and as the warrior bore in, he landed a hard right to the Indian's belly. The man backed up a step, then leaped for the sheriff, managing to get a hold on his shirt and dragging him to the dirt.

Horton butted the Indian in the face again, and this time the big man screamed in pain. The lawman threw a short, hard punch that caught the warrior in the throat and gave Horton enough time to get back to his feet.

Horton crouched and circled the Indian, seeking a way to end the fight quickly. His vision was dim and breath rasped in his throat. His lungs were on fire from his exertions. The Indian was bleeding heavily from the nose and mouth, but he looked more determined than ever. He had dropped his knife.

The lawman stepped in and threw a left to the body that landed just below the heart and followed it with a wild right cross that missed, throwing him off balance. The Indian clubbed him behind the ear with a big, iron-hard fist, and threw him into the dirt.

Horton struggled to get back on his feet. His ears rang from the blow, and he couldn't seem to catch his breath. He watched as the Indian swooped up his knife and lunged at him. He twisted his body and felt the blade slice across his chest, opening a wound nearly a foot long. The sheriff swung a right that missed, then slipped and fell to his knees.

Horton saw the look of triumph in the big Indian's eyes, then watched as the expression changed to one of wonder and then to the glassy stare of death. He saw Duncan pull his Arkansas Toothpick from the man's back as the warrior toppled forward lifelessly.

"Come on, Matt," the kid said as he helped Horton to his feet. "They've pulled back again, but they won't wait very long. We gotta get out of here while we got the chance."

Horton nodded dumbly, too exhausted to speak. He looked around and found his Colt, picked it up and re-loaded as fast as his trembling fingers would allow. He accepted the Winchester that Duncan handed him, reloaded it, too, and allowed himself to be led to the horses.

Duncan managed to catch one of the dead Comanches' horses and he mounted it as Horton swung onto the roan. The big horse seemed to have gathered some strength from their brief halt and, no longer being asked to carry double, seemed almost eager to be on his way again.

The two men headed for the station, wondering what they would find there.

Pedro had long since put down the shotgun and had taken up the Winchester. He fired at any target that presented itself, but he had little hope of hitting anything. He was a poor shot with a rifle or a handgun, but a Comanche laying in front of the station, nearly cut in half from a blast from the shotgun, spoke of the proprietor's prowess with that weapon. But after the initial rush, the Indians had retreated into the brush, far beyond the range of O'Brien's Greener.

Harry had dropped one warrior as he had attempted to rush the building, and he had killed a horse after missing its rider. Jack thought that he might have gotten some lead into one or two of the warriors, but with only one hand, and his left one at that, he could only fire a pistol, and the Indians had not remained in range for long.

The trio were well-situated, however. They were pro-tected by adobe walls four feet thick, they had enough ammunition and rifles to outfit a small battalion, and there were food, water, and beer enough to last them for months.

The situation was not as good as they would have liked, however. Three men were not enough to cover all sides of the building at once. Two men on each of the long sides and one man on each end might have done the job if no one had needed to eat or sleep, but with only three people, they had to constantly shift firing positions in order to discourage those who would try to sneak up on them. This system would work fairly well in daylight, but darkness would be a different matter. There was no way that they could visually cover all of the ground around them.

They had another worry, too. The roof of the station was made of cedar shingles that had been baked under the blazing sun for a dozen years. One fire arrow would turn their fortress into a blazing inferno. But to shoot that arrow, the archer would have to get close to the station, much closer than the edge of the cleared strip. Pedro thought that they could keep the Comanches out of range during the day. It was the thought of night and all that it threatened that bothered him,

Pedro moved to the window behind the bar and looked out through the firing port in the shutter. At first, he saw nothing, but then something attracted his attention. He could have sworn that the lone cedar tree at the edge of the clearing was now closer to the building than it had been the last time he had checked. Even as he watched it, he saw it move slightly forward. He watched a little longer and saw it move again more boldly.

Pedro called out softly to Harry.

"I've got a tree over here that moves. It's about two hundred and fifty yards away, Harry. At that range I would miss a man. You want to give it a try?"

Harry came over to the firing post and took a look. The tree did not move.

"You sure that tree moved?" he asked.

"I cut every damn tree down myself," Pedro answered, "an' I got the scars to prove it. That cedar didn't just grow there this afternoon. Besides, I seen it move. Twice."

Harry said nothing but slipped his rifle into the port. He sighted low, not more than a foot or so from the bottom of the tree and fired. The tree quivered and rocked a little. Harry fired twice more, aiming higher each time. The tree fell and a warrior pitched forward, dead. Harry fed three more cartridges into the rifle to replace those that he'd fired, then went back to his window without a word.

Pedro looked back through the firing port and jerked his head back quickly as a bullet struck the shutters hard, plowing through the tough wood and sending splinters flying. It would take nearly six inches of wood to completely stop a slug fired from that range, and the shutters were barely two inches thick. Pedro wished that he's gone with his wife to purchase supplies and had left his hired man behind. He vowed that if he lived through this, he'd do that next time. But first there had to be a next time.

It was Harry who first gave the alarm.

"We got riders comin' in from the south," he yelled as he slipped his rifle into firing position. A minute later he added, "They're white men. I think one of 'ems that fella we tangled with here a few days ago."

Jack rushed to the window and took a look. "That's the bastard who smashed my hand!" he exclaimed as he backed into the middle of the room.

There was firing outside as the riders broke into the cleared strip and the Comanches saw what was happening. Harry started giving covering fire and Pedro took the bar off the door and opened it wide. Then he ran back to his window and began spraying lead into the brush.

Bullets were thick as the two riders thundered up to the station and leaped to the ground. Duncan came through the door in a rush, followed closely by Horton.

The first thing Horton saw when he ran into Cedar Station was that damn-fool gunman who he had fought the last time he was there. He was standing in the middle of the room, bandaged right hand high in the air, and his left hovering over a gun butt.

"I'm going to kill you, you son of a bitch!" Jack screamed as he went for his gun.

Time seemed to stand still for Horton. He heard Pedro start to yell, whether to warn Horton or to distract the gunman he could not tell. The sheriff clawed for his Colt, knowing as his hand touched its butt that he would not be fast enough this time. Nevertheless, he completed his draw and thumbed back the hammer as he brought the gun to bear. He watched as the gunman's Colt spit smoke and flame, and he felt a tremendous blow strike him in the chest.

Horton started to fall. On his way to the floor, he saw the gunman fire again and felt the wind from the slug as it whipped past his head. Then he fired his own Colt just as blackness swept over him. He heard a high-pitched scream and then he was falling into a bottomless pit. He never felt himself hit the floor.

Chapter 17

Spotted Calf stopped the war party at the edge of the clearing and watched as the door to the station slammed shut and the two horses, now riderless, trotted off. He signaled for his band to spread out and encircle the building, then he set off in search of Yellow Horse.

He found him on the far side of the circle, talking with a group of young warriors. When he saw his father, Yellow Horse broke off his conversation and swiftly walked over to him.

"The trading post still stands," Spotted Calf observed. "Why has it not been burned?"

"We did not take them by surprise, my father," Yellow horse answered. "And there are several defenders inside. We have lost four of our number dead and two more are wounded because of their rifles. We were trying to decide how to get close enough to the building to set it afire when you came. We are glad that you are here and can now help us find a way to force Swift Eagle from his lair."

Spotted Calf looked at his son for a long moment. He wondered if this was another of his son's lame excuses for failure. At that moment a rifle in the station fired and he felt the bullet strike a powerful blow in the left leg, a blow that was hard enough to spin him around and knock him to the ground.

Yellow Horse grabbed his father under the arms and dragged him deeper into the brush. He laid his father in a shallow fold in the ground and then inspected the wound.

The bullet that struck Spotted Calf had penetrated his left thigh from the back and had gone completely through the leg and out the front, taking with it a piece of flesh about the size of a goose egg. Yellow Horse bound the wound as best he could. It was not a good job, but it did staunch the flow of the blood. The young warrior saw that it was a bad wound, but that it could have been much worse. The large thigh bone had not been broken, and Yellow Horse breathed easier. He thought that his father would survive.

Spotted Calf was beginning to feel a great burning pain in his leg, now that the first numbing shock of the wound had worn off. The pain would get worse—much worse—before it got better, he knew. This was his fourth wound from bullets, and there had been others as well, wounds caused by arrows and lances and knives. These were the result of a life spent as a warrior. He had survived the others, and he would survive this one now. The spirits had always smiled upon him,

Yellow Horse looked at the sun and saw that it would not be long before it would be night. The skyline was already turning crimson in anticipation. The young warrior turned to his father for guidance.

"Father, we have not long before it becomes dark. What would you have us do?"

Spotted Calf pushed the pain from his mind. He raised himself on his elbows and looked up at his son.

"Try once more to take the buildings," he said. "Take all of the warriors and attack from all sides at once. Have some of our braves take the horses they keep in the building and in the stone circle. Wait until the sun sinks just below the hills. Then they will not be able to see as well as you." Slowly he sank back to the ground, his strength spent.

Yellow Horse needed nothing more from his father. He went around the circle that the war party had formed around the buildings and told the warriors what they were to do, He was surprised at the number of warriors that were missing, He thought that there must be nearly thirty men gone, men who would be lying dead or wounded on the plain, sacrificed so that Swift Eagle would die for the murder of Running Buffalo.

Yellow horse felt shame and guilt that so many men, including his own father, should be dead or wounded when he could have prevented it all just by killing Swift Eagle the first time he had seen him. Then this chase would never have happened, and no one would have been hurt. There would be many women and children wailing and crying around the cook fires because he had made the wrong decision, because his courage had wavered at the critical moment. He vowed that he would not waver again. Swift Eagle would die. He promised that to the spirits of his fallen warriors. And if the spirits smiled upon him, he, Yellow Horse, would be the one who would take Swift Eagle's life.

The young warrior completed his preparations and found a spot where he could look upon the door that Swift Eagle had used to enter the station. He waited patiently for the sun to sink below the horizon. It seemed to hang above the hills forever, but finally there was only the smallest edge of the sun to be seen. Yellow Horse sighted his father's rifle on the door and fired. Immediately he and the rest of the war party were on their feet, running as fast as they could for the buildings, their war cries piercing the evening air, The battle was joined.

Horton opened his eyes, not sure of what he would find. The pain let him know that he was not dead. He tried to sit up, but his vision began to swim, and he gave up his attempt, at least for the moment.

He looked around the station and found that he was lying on Pedro's bunk. He saw Tommy across the room, peering through a firing port. The young gunman that he had slugged with his Colt a few days before was keeping watch from another port behind the bar, and

Pedro was near a third window, covering the door that he and Duncan had used to enter the station.

There was no trace of the gunman who had shot him. Horton wondered idly where he had gone.

The sheriff was becoming more aware of his surroundings, in spite of the failing light. The lanterns would not be lit tonight, for light would make it impossible to see anything outside the building. He decided to try once more to sit up. This time he was successful, and he swung his feet to the floor quickly, before he could change his mind. His head swam again for a moment and then cleared, but he did not try to stand. He was too weak to try that just yet.

Pedro looked over and saw that the sheriff was awake and sitting up. He leaned his rifle against the wall and walked over to his friend.

"It's good to see you back among the living, my friend," he said, his face wreathed in a smile. "We thought for a little while that you were a goner."

Horton tried to smile and said, "I thought I was, too. When I saw that gunman's Colt flame, I thought that I was lookin' into the back door of hell." Horton paused for a second or two and then added, "Where is that jasper, anyway?"

Pedro, still grinning from ear to ear, said, "He's behind the bar. We rolled him up in a blanket an' put him there until things quiet down a little."

"He's dead, then," Horton said with finality. "I didn't think I'd hit him. Must of been a lucky shot."

"Oh, you hit him, all right," Pedro said, "but you didn't kill him. Harry did that job for you. Your shot hit that coyote right plumb center in that busted-up hand of his. You could have heard him scream all the way into El Paso. I ain't never heard nothin' like it. I hope that I never hear nothin' like it again, neither."

"Harry?" Horton asked. "Who in hell is Harry?" Then light dawned for the sheriff. "I must be gettin' slow. Harry's that dead gent's partner, right?"

"Maybe 'partner' is too strong a word, Matt," the proprietor answered. "They was together when they got here, but Harry's the only reason I'm still alive an' kickin'. That man Jack had me lookin' down the barrel of the Colt of his an' wishin' to be anywhere but here. Harry threatened to shoot him if he didn't leave me alone, an' Jack backed down. I want to tell you that I was real scared."

"Don't blame you none, Pedro," Matt said. "I owe him life, too, it seems like. What's happenin' outside? How long was I out?"

This time it was Duncan who spoke up. "You was out for not more than an hour, maybe less, Matt. The only thing we can see outside is some movin' around in the brush. We got lots of ammo, so we pepper the bushes some when we see movement. Then we change windows an' have at 'em again. Damn boring, if you was to ask me."

"You won't be bored if that bunch decides to rush this place," Horton said. "There must be a hundred of 'em."

"Some less 'n that, Matt," Tommy corrected. "I think that we hurt 'em bad in them two run-ins we had with 'em. In fact, I'm surprised that they haven't packed it up an' gone home. It ain't like them to keep on so when they ain't doin' much good an' their losses have been high."

Horton said softly, "I reckon they think they got cause to stick around, Tommy. They want you so bad they can taste it. An' I think that the rest of us are none too popular with 'em, either. Like you said, we hurt 'em some today."

Pedro interrupted. "You better shut up an' get some rest, Matt. You took quite a hit from Jack."

"What's it look like, Pedro?" Matt asked as he glanced at the bandage on his chest.

"The gunshot was high up, my friend, an' as far as I can see it didn't hit a bone or any major veins or your lungs. The slug went clean through you, so I didn't even have to poke around lookin' for it. But you still got you two good-sized holes through your hide. That knife cut was pretty bad, too. It was close to an inch deep in some places. I washed out those holes an' cuts with some bar whiskey an' sewed up the cut. Harry put the bandage on you. You owe me for the cloth used, by the way. An' even if you're really a big man an' twice as tough as you think you are, you're gonna be sore as hell an' weaker 'n a cat for quite a spell."

Horton grinned thinly and said, "Pedro, I thank you an' Harry an' Tommy, too, for patchin' me up. But now you'd better put a chair over by that window an' put me in it. I'd take it as a favor if you'd give me some ammo an' my Winchester. In fact, Pedro, you can give me back my brother's Henry, too. I can still shoot some, an' if an' when those Comanches come a-runnin', we're gonna need every gun we got."

Pedro and Duncan started protesting, but Horton cut off all discussion.

"Look, friends, I know that you're only tryin' to take care of me, but if those Comanches rush us an' get inside, my scalp's gonna end up on a stick, same as yours. If I'm gonna die, I want it to be with a rifle in my hands. Now suppose we cut out the talkin' an' get me moved over to a window while we still got the time?"

Pedro and Duncan didn't like it, but they could not fault Horton's thinking. They put out a chair at the end of the building and dragged a table over close to it. Then they gently carried the sheriff to the firing port and put him in the chair. After they wrapped him up good in a blanket, they brought over the rifles and ammunition he wanted. Pedro then brought over a shotgun, two boxes of shells for it, a tall glass of beer, and some beans that were cooling fast.

"You'd better try to eat a little," the proprietor said. "If you can't keep this down, I'll get you a can of peaches an' you can drink the juice."

"You gonna put 'em on my bill, too?" Horton joked.

"You must be feelin' better," Pedro said, "tryin' to make a joke. There ain't no question about puttin' that stuff on your bill. Of course I am, an' I'm gonna put what ammo you use on there, too, so be careful how you shoot."

"That's what I've always admired about you, Pedro," Horton said. "You're the champion of free enterprise. Anyway, I'd rather owe you than beat you out of it."

Pedro laughed and went back to his firing port. It was quiet outside, too quiet for comfort. Horton heard some bird calls and wondered if the birds that made them had beaks or bows. He saw some movement in the brush and resisted the temptation to fire. He decided that he did not have enough strength to do a whole lot of shooting and reloading, and besides, he wanted the Comanches to believe that this end of the building was unguarded. They might get a little careless if they thought that no one was looking, and Horton wanted any advantage that he could get.

The sheriff had lived in Texas all his life, except for the time he was back east during the war, and he had more than his share of experience with the Comanche. There was not a more fierce, more proud, or more dangerous adversary anywhere in the state. These people were not just going to fade away during the night. Barring some kind of miracle, this was going to be a fight to the finish, and in the end the Comanche would win. There were just too many of them for these four men to hold off indefinitely. Sooner or later, they'd storm the place, and it would be all over but the dying, dying that would be quick if they were lucky and slow and painful if they were not.

Horton checked his big Colt pistol again and then asked Pedro if he had any more handguns around. Pedro brought over Jack's gun belts and laid them on the table, then went back to his vantage point. Horton felt better, knowing that the extra pistols were there. If the Indians once got inside the building, rifles would not be worth much.

The sheriff checked Jack's pistols and reloaded the two chambers that had been fired at him. It gave Horton a funny feeling to be handling the gun that had nearly killed him. When he finished, he slumped back in his chair, more tired than he could remember ever having been before. And as much as he hated to admit it, the waiting was getting to him. He willed for something to happen soon, before it got too dark to see. He knew in his bones that the Comanche would attack at dusk. If they did not manage to take the building, they would try again at dawn, and they'd keep at it until the job was done.

Horton heard the rifle shot and the thud of the slug as it tore through the door and buried itself in the opposite wall. Then there came the war cries and figures running across the clearing. The sheriff rested the muzzle of his Winchester on the firing port and began firing rapidly, aiming carefully each time before squeezing the trigger. Warrior after warrior fell, but still they came on. These warriors were determined. It would be a fight to the finish.

Horton heard the others firing as well, a constant thundering as rifles spat death into the twilight. Bullets thudded into the walls and shutters as the Indians fired from the protection of the brush and from uneven folds in the ground.

There were screams of pain coming from the wounded, and soon the Comanches were close enough so that Horton could see the expressions on their faces as the slugs ripped into their flesh, and he remembered that not long ago it was his flesh that had been struck. He fired again and again, and the barrel of his Winchester grew hot to the touch. More men fell into twisted heaps in the dust.

But the Comanches kept on coming.

Chapter 18

Yellow Horse yelled with the rest of the warriors as they ran as fast as they could for the station. Bullets flew everywhere, and the sound of lead striking living flesh filled the air. Occasionally warriors screamed in pain as they fell; others simply crumbled to the ground, dead or dying, Yellow Horse felt a bullet tug at his vest and his hand went numb as a bullet struck the receiver of the rifle he carried. He dropped the useless weapon and ran on, amazed at his good fortune. The bullet would have struck him in the chest if it had not hit the rifle. The spirits were protecting him, he thought. Tonight, victory surely would be his,

But many warriors would pay the price for that victory. At least twenty more men had fallen, and the war party had still not crossed the open area in front of the station. Suddenly Yellow Horse found himself alone, the others either dead, dying, or breaking for the mesquite and cedar they had just left. He was alone, and he could hear and feel the bullets whip past him as he ran and dodged, praying that he could make it to the wall before he was struck down.

And then he was at the wall. He flattened himself against it, knowing that he was out of the sight of the defenders.

He was also without a weapon. The knife in his belt was all that he had, and it was useless against the building. He looked for something, for anything, that he could use to break into the building, but he saw nothing.

The rifle protruding from the window continued to spit flame as the defenders sought new targets. Yellow Horse was enraged. He reached out, grabbed the barrel, and pulled as hard as he could. He heard a cry of surprise from within the building, and then he was on the ground, a new Winchester in his hands. He rolled back against the wall, safe again from the fire from within.

Yellow Horse got to his feet and cried out to his companions. He levered a fresh cartridge into the chamber, aimed into the firing port, and fired. He was rewarded with a cry of pain, but he was too busy to pay any attention to that. He fired as fast as he could lever cartridges into the chamber and pull the trigger.

And then the hammer fell and the firing pin had no cartridge in front of it. The rifle was empty. Yellow Horse flattened himself against the wall again, waiting to see if anyone would be foolish enough to stick another rifle through the port. As he waited, several warriors joined him against the wall. Some had fallen and pretended to be dead in order to escape the fire from the station, others had run back from the brush while

Yellow Horse had been firing through the gun port. All had rallied on the young warrior when they saw his bravery and determination.

One of the braves had a rifle and a bandolier of ammunition in the same caliber as the rifle that Yellow Horse carried. He took some cartridges and reloaded his weapon, then looked for a way to use it most effectively.

"Yellow Horse," a brave named Angry Cougar said, "We must set this place afire. How can we do this?"

Yellow Horse thought about how this could be done. He had no flint, but others might. What he needed most was tinder.

"Follow the walls to the side that faces the bar. I will shoot into the hole as you run. We will find tinder there, and someone will have a bow. We will burn out Swift Eagle and his friends."

The men made their way around the building, crawling low beneath the shuttered windows. Finally, they were ready to make a break for the corral and the barn behind it. Yellow Horse could see that the horses had been released from the corral and that firing that came from the barn told him that his warriors had made it at least that far before slowing their attack.

Yellow Horse and the other warrior with a rifle stood on either side of a firing port and, on a signal from the young warrior, began firing into the station as the others made a dash for the corral. From there they could run in a crouch to the barn, safe from any fire from the station.

Suddenly a pistol spoke from the other firing port along that wall of the station and one of Yellow Horse's warriors threw his hands into the air, bent backwards, and screamed in pain as he fell to the ground, mortally wounded. Yellow Horse dashed to that firing port and fired into it—once, twice, three times.

And then he heard a cry from the corral. It was time for them to make a break for it, too. Yellow Horse signaled to the other brave with a rifle, and they both fired into the ports twice more and then ran as fast as they could for the corral. No one fired at them as they ran,

The two warriors waited for a few minutes to catch their breath, then crouched low and ran for the safety of the barn. They made it through the doorway and into the gloom of the building.

Yellow Horse saw that here, too, the horses had been released. There were nearly twenty braves either in the barn or around it. No one had defended the barn, and no warrior had been hurt in its capture. Yellow Horse knew that these warriors had been fortunate. The gunfire on the other three sides had been murderous.

Quickly Yellow Horse and the other braves made fire arrows while Angry Cougar started a small fire in the corner of the barn. As soon as the station was well alight, they would set fire to the barn as well, then wait in the bush for the defenders to either burn to death or try to make a run for it, Yellow Horse hoped that Swift Eagle would try to run. They would catch him then, and Swift Eagle would die slowly, painfully, until he begged for death.

Angry Cougar snapped Yellow Horse from his reverie.

"The arrows are ready, Yellow Horse. Will you give me the honor of the first shot?"

Yellow Horse took a bow from the brave standing next to him and picked up an arrow.

"We shall have the honor together," he said. "We do this thing for the honor of my father and for the spirits of Running Buffalo and all those who died hunting Swift Eagle."

The two warriors stuck their arrows into the fire until the tinder caught, then stepped to the doorway and fired their arrows at the roof of the station. As soon as they fired, they stepped back inside the safety of the building and picked up fresh arrows as others made their way to the doorway to shoot. Soon there were more than a dozen blazing arrows embedded in the roof. Yellow Horse watched as the flames took hold and spread rapidly. He knew that Spotted Calf watched, too, and he was filled with pride.

He took another arrow, stuck it into the fire, and waited until it was burning brightly. Then he tossed it into the hay and watched as it burst into flame.

"Come, my brothers," Yellow Horse said to the other warriors. "It is time for us to leave here. Circle again the buildings, and if anyone comes out, kill them. And if you see Swift Eagle come out, try to capture him alive. He should be a present to my father."

The warriors whooped in reply as they ran out from the back of the barn and into the brush, hidden now in the increasing darkness and the flickering shadows cast by the dancing flames from the roof of the station.

It had been Pedro who had shouted in surprise when the Winchester had been torn from his hands, and it had also been he who had yelled in pain as Yellow Horse's shot through the firing port had blown off the upper third of his right ear. Blood poured from the wound as he tried to staunch the flow with a shirt from the counter next to him. He finally succeeded in fashioning a bandage of sorts while Yellow Horse was busy spraying the inside of the station with lead. Fortunately, no one else was hit.

Pedro cut loose with a stream of oaths and then said something else. All was lost to the other three men, for none of them spoke Spanish, at least not well enough to follow the river of words pouring from Pedro.

"Whoa there, Pedro," Tommy said. "Speak slower or in English, one or the other. I can't keep up with you."

Pedro started again, in English. "They are against the walls, these Comanches. I did not build this place with that in mind. There is no way that we can get a shot at them. What'll we do?"

Harry pulled back from his window for a minute and said, "'Pears to me it ain't what we're gonna do but what they're gonna do. The walls is too thick to push in an' the doors an' windows are too thick. I'd guess that they're gonna either chop a hole in the roof or set it on fire. I don't see what else they could do."

Horton thought about what Harry had to say, then spoke.

"Pedro, did you plan for fire when you built this place?" he asked.

"As a matter of fact, Matt, I did. Down under the bar is a pit I dug. I keep the beer in it to keep it cold."

"Beggin' your pardon, Pedro, but right now we don't need a cold beer," Tommy interrupted. "What we need is a way outta here."

"An' that's what you'll have if you'll shut up long enough to let me finish," Pedro said with considerable feeling. "I dug a tunnel from that pit out to the corral. You remember that the water trough out there is about three feet off the ground. Well, the tunnel comes out under the trough. There's planks an' about a foot of dirt over the hole, but it's there just the same."

"Then I suggest," said Horton, "that we get ready to use that tunnel. Harry, why don't you an' Pedro grab what we're gonna need an' put it in the pit while Tommy an' I keep an eye out for trouble." Everyone understood that what the sheriff had said was not a question but was rather a polite order.

"Good idea," Harry said as he walked over to the ammunition shelves and started putting boxes of cartridges into a sack. "I'm betting that we ain't got that much time before them Comanches try somethin' else."

Pedro moved the body of Jack back into the room and then opened up the trap door behind the bar and started dropping down into the pit the sacks of ammunition and food that Harry brought over to him. Then he went over to the dry goods counter and, after a moment or two spent in thought, selected some clothes and threw them in the pit, too.

"You goin' to a fancy-dress ball, Pedro?" Horton asked. "What's with the clothes?"

"If you could see yourself, amigo, you wouldn't ask." the proprietor answered. "You an' Duncan look like scarecrows, an' I got more blood on my shirt than I got in my veins. We'll need the clothes when this is over, mark my words."

The conversation was interrupted by a fusillade of shots from the side of the building closest to the stables.

"They're at the ports again!" Harry shouted. "Hit the floor!"

The others dropped low, but Horton just crouched a little lower in his chair. He feared that if he ever got on the floor, he'd be unable to get up again,

"Tommy!" he yelled. "Catch the other window on the stable side. They're up to somethin'."

Tommy ran across the room and took a quick look through the firing port, then drew a pistol and snapped off a shot. He was rewarded with a scream as the Comanche at whom he had aimed fell to the ground. He flattened himself against the wall as more bullets came tearing through the firing port, then waited a few seconds before taking another look. He saw two or three Indians disappear into the barn, and he could have sworn that one of them had been Yellow Horse. He reported what he had seen.

Horton thought for a moment, then got unsteadily to his feet. Tommy came over to give him a hand, but the sheriff motioned him aside.

"Harry hit it right, I think," the lawman said. "In about five minutes this place will be on fire. Get the rifles an' let's be goin' while the gettin' is good."

First Harry and then Pedro jumped into the pit. Tommy stood by as Horton made his way slowly across the room and moved behind the bar. From time to time a bullet blasted its way through a door or a shutter, but by the time Horton was ready to allow himself to be lowered into the pit they heard the sound of arrows striking the roof. Within moments faint streams of smoke began to sift into the room.

"It won't be long now," Horton said. "Lower me gently."

Tommy eased the sheriff into the pit, then dropped down, too, pulling the trap door closed as he went. Pedro had a pair of candles burning and put them on a ledge. He moved two barrels aside, revealing another door.

"Sure hope there ain't no rats or snakes or nuthin' in here," the big man said. "I haven't been in here for years."

"Now you tell us," Tommy grumbled. Horton glared at him.

"Whatever's in there won't give us near the hot reception we was gonna get upstairs. Let's get goin'."

Pedro opened the door and revealed a tunnel about four feet high and three feet wide. He threw a bung hammer down the tunnel, but nothing ran out and they did not hear anything. Still, Pedro hesitated.

"What's the holdup?" Horton demanded.

"Nuthin'," Pedro answered. I just wanted to give the critters a chance to leave if they wanted to."

Harry grabbed a candle, pushed past the proprietor, and entered the tunnel on his hands and knees. Tommy followed close behind. Pedro came back to Matt and helped him into the tunnel, then tossed in the sacks of supplies before he shut the door behind him. As a last gesture he barred the door, just in case someone tried to follow.

Up ahead Harry came to the end of the tunnel. There were a pair of steps leading nowhere. He crawled up on them and stood up slowly, pressing his back against the boards that formed the roof of the tunnel. Slowly the boards gave way, and dirt fell down on him as he poked his head above ground level. Pedro had been right. The water trough was directly overhead.

The corral was empty and the gate was open. Harry snuffed out his candle and removed the planks covering the tunnel exit, then pulled himself over the lip and crawled out into the corral. The light from the burning buildings cast eerie shadows over the stone enclosure, and Harry thought that he had never felt so exposed in his life.

He moved quickly to the wall of the corral and crouching, followed it to the gate. He lowered himself to his belly and peered around the wall.

He saw several figures running through the brush, but he was not tempted to shoot. The Comanches did not know they were there, and as far as he was concerned, he'd like to keep it that way.

He saw Tommy moving along the wall opposite him. He, too, stopped at the gate opening and lowered himself to the ground. Before long Horton crawled out from under the trough and propped himself up against one end of it. Pedro emerged last and took up a position at the opposite end of the trough from Horton. They all settled in to wait.

It promised to be a long night.

Chapter 19

Yellow Horse watched the station burn. The flames from the barn had subsided quickly once the hay had been consumed, but the trading post continued to burn brightly. The roof fell in, sending a shower of sparks high into the air. From time-to-time ammunition went off as flames reached crates that Pedro had stashed in various places in the station. Yellow Horse and the rest of the warriors were mesmerized by the spectacle.

The young warrior sought out his father. Spotted Calf was resting as comfortably as possible where he had parted with his son earlier in the day. Someone had made a back rest for him from cut branches and blankets, and a low fire burned nearby, giving light and the impression of warmth. Yellow Horse approached his father and prepared to tell him what had happened.

"Come, sit here beside me, my son, and tell me what has happened," the old man said. "I no longer hear firing. Have you captured Swift Eagle?"

Yellow Horse sat down next to his father and studied him for a moment or two before answering. He saw that his father's face was drawn with pain, but the wound no longer bled and his eyes were bright. Yellow Horse chose his words carefully.

"The attack is finished, father. The barn and the trading post have been set on fire, and all of the horses are now numbered with our own. The trading post still burns brightly, and things keep exploding. We know that there were at least four men in the trading post. I myself saw that one of them was Swift Eagle. The roof of the trading post has fallen to the flames. No one left the building, father. No one will ever leave the building."

"And what was the cost, son?" the old man asked.

"I do not know exactly, father, but about half of those who began this hunt for Swift Eagle are either dead or wounded. I will not know the true number until after we go back over our path and we see who among those who fell earlier in the day still live."

"You have spoken well, my son," Spotted Calf said. "The cost has been high, but the murder of Running Buffalo has been avenged." The old man looked at his son and continued, "And you have become a man at last." He clasped his son's arm and squeezed gently.

"I do not know what to say, father," Yellow Horse said truthfully.

"Then say nothing, my son. Have someone keep watch on the trading post tonight. Tomorrow we will see the bodies of our enemies and then go back to our people. There will be trouble with the horse soldiers because of this, so we must move our people north, away from here."

"I will see that it is done, father, and will see also to our dead. And the rest of the warriors I will bring back here to eat and drink and tell of what has happened this day. Many were very brave, and none more so than Angry Cougar. He was of great help to me in the final battle."

The old man grunted and nodded his head in approval. Yellow Horse stood up and went off to do as his father had ordered. Spotted Calf was pleased for many reasons, not the least of which was the fact that his son had shared his honor with another brave, Angry Cougar. That was something he would not have done even two days ago.

The old man lay back and rested as warriors began gathering around him. Soon much of the brush had been cleared from around them and a larger fire had been started. Food and water were brought out, and the men began to eat and talk. Laughter was heard, and the old warrior knew that the battle was truly over.

But the battle was not over for the four men in the stone corral.

When Pedro and his hired man had built the corral, they had defense in mind. The walls were nearly six feet high and there were firing ports all the way around the wall. The original gate had been solid wood, but it had been replaced a long time ago with one made of widely separated slats of wood, an arrangement that was light and easy to handle but which offered little protection. Just then Pedro wished that the original gate was still there, firmly closed.

Tommy Duncan crawled over to Horton and said softly, "'Pears to me that the Comanche think we're still in the station. Maybe we'd better light out of here now before they learn different,"

Horton shook his head and said, "We'd not get far, Tommy. We've got no horses an' I couldn't go a mile even with help. They'd find us in the mornin' an' we'd be caught in the open with no protection at all. Besides, you an' I both know that there's braves out there right now just waitin' for someone to move."

"Maybe you're right, Matt, an' maybe you ain't," the younger man answered, "but it's for sure that they'll find out in the mornin' that there's only one body in that tradin' post. It won't take 'em long to look in here, an' then it'll be the Alamo all over again. I think we better leave now an' take our chances."

Horton thought for a few minutes while Duncan waited impatiently. He finally came to a decision and turned again to Tommy.

"You talk with the others," he said, "an' if they're of like mind, then you can go. I'm stayin' here. Maybe I can get back in the tunnel an' they won't find me. What's sure is that I ain't up to travel, fast or otherwise.

An' to tell you the truth, I don't believe Pedro is, either. He's a good man but he's a hundred pounds too fat, an' he's soft besides. Now go talk to the others an' tell me what you decide."

Tommy looked at Horton. He saw a man in great pain. Even in the shadow of the corral wall, he could see that the sheriff was all used up. Horton had spoken wisely and truthfully.

"There's no need to talk to the others," Tommy said finally. "Either we all go or we all stay. But I think that there may be another way to go."

"What have you got in mind?" Horton asked.

"It's me that Yellow Horse is after. It has always been me. They don't care nuthin' about you an' Pedro an' Harry. Now, just suppose that I was to skin out of here and pay a little call on their camp. I can steal a horse as good as any Comanche, an' I could let myself be seen long enough to be recognized an' then head for the border. They'd follow, surer'n hell. The weekly stage'll be through here about noon tomorrow an' pick you up an' take you back to Benton. An' I won't get my neck stretched. That'd work out for everybody."

"You wouldn't get your neck stretched, Tommy," the sheriff said. "You'd get an arrow in your back. You said it yourself. Either we all go or none of us goes."

"I think you're wrong, Matt. I can pull it off with a little luck. We're all goin' to die in the mornin' anyway, so what've we got to lose? A few hours one way or the other ain't nuthin'. Besides, I owe you somethin' for gettin' you in this fix."

"You might pull it off, an' then again you might not. You're right that if it didn't work it wouldn't change what's goin' to happen to us anyway. But I don't want you takin' that kind of risk for me. It's a matter of honor."

"Damn your honor, Matt!" Duncan spat. "Are you gonna let these other men die because of your honor?"

"There's been a lot of good men who died here today for honor," the lawman said with feeling. "Three or four more won't make any difference."

Duncan swore softly. "There's no arguin' with you. You've been a hard-headed bastard ever since I met you. I don't know why I ever tried to talk sense into you."

"I don't know either, Tommy. Now why don't you just shut up an' go back up there by the gate? I've enjoyed all of this conversation that I can stand for one night."

Duncan was mad clear through. He was talking sense and Horton was being a proud, honorable fool. He started to tell him so, then gave up in disgust and crawled back to the place he had vacated by the gate. Harry looked at him questioningly and Tommy just shrugged. That seemed to be good enough for Harry.

Tommy lay there for better than two hours before the flames from the trading post had died down far enough for his purpose. Silently he unbuckled his gun belt. He put the gun and the belt together in a small pile, then added his hold-out pistol. He had promised Horton that he would not use his guns to escape, and he wouldn't. He'd show Matt that he knew something about honor, too. He wished that he still had his moccasins, but he'd have to do without them. He waited until Harry looked the other way, then he slipped out of the mouth of the corral and into the darkness. To hell with Horton and his honor, he thought. Tonight, he would do what was right.

No one saw Tommy leave, even Harry, who was lying only a few feet away. He turned back to check on Duncan and saw that he was gone. He had no idea what had happened, but he knew that he'd better let Horton know. He crawled over to him as fast as he could without making any noise.

"Duncan's gone," he whispered. "One minute he was there an' the next he wasn't. What do you think we ought to do?"

Somehow Horton was not surprised. Tommy had always done what he thought was best, and somewhere deep inside he hoped that the kid would make it.

"There's nuthin' we can do, Harry," he whispered back. "You'd never find him out there, so don't even think of tryin'. For now, you'd better go back to where you was an' keep watch. In an hour or so, wake Pedro an' then get some sleep. I'll pull the last watch. We'll see some action around sunup, or I'll miss my guess."

Harry crawled back to his spot by the gate and peered out into the darkness. At first, he saw nothing, but then he saw a figure move against the dull glow of the burned-out station. The figure was moving slowly towards the corral. Harry could not tell if it was Tommy or a Comanche, but he was not going to take any chances. He stood up slowly and flattened himself against the wall of the corral.

The figure kept coming. He moved with agility and seemed to be unconcerned about any possible danger. He walked straight into the mouth of the corral, then stopped.

"Tommy?" Harry whispered.

He was answered with a knife blade that he did not quite avoid. He felt the fire of the blade as it raked across his ribs, and he groped frantically for the Comanche's wrist. He somehow managed to grab it in time to stop a second thrust, then he found himself being tripped up and falling. He held onto the warrior's wrist as he fell and managed to roll over on top of his attacker. While he held the brave's wrist with one hand, he chopped blindly with the other at his advisory's throat. He heard the warrior choking and he somehow got a knee on the man's arm, pinning the hand with the knife to the ground. He got both hands on the warrior's throat and squeezed with all his might. The man fought back, but very quickly the strength went out of him and he was dead. Then Pedro was beside him, helping him to his feet.

He stood there, trembling. He had never killed a man with his bare hands before, and it had shaken him badly. It had been so personal. He had felt the man's breath against his face and felt the life as it was choked from him. He turned aside and retched quietly.

"You did good, Harry," Pedro whispered. "You didn't make a sound. We're safe, thanks to you."

"Not for long," Harry managed to say. "He was a guard, an' someone'll come to take his place. When they can't find him, they'll start lookin' hard. Then they'll find us."

Pedro did not have a comeback for that. He just nodded and found a place near the gate that suited him. He sat with his back against the wall and tried not to think about what would happen when the warrior was found missing.

Chapter 20

Tommy Duncan was afraid. He'd been afraid before, but not like this. He was going into the Comanche camp, and the odds were fifty to one that he would come out alive.

When he left the corral, he had headed west, first moving slowly on his belly and then more rapidly, crouching as he moved among the patches of cedar and mesquite. He could hear and smell the horse herd long before he could see it. He studied the area and decided that there were only two warriors guarding the herd, and they were none too alert. He started to circle north, to get behind the guard there, kill him silently with his knife, and then stampede the herd through the Comanche camp about two hundred yards to the south. Then he was going to head for the border just as fast as his horse could take him.

But Tommy began to have second thoughts even before he began to move in on the guard. It was bad enough that he was hunted for a bank robbery, something he had done, but it was intolerable that he should be hunted for a murder that he had not done. He decided that he would sneak into the Indian camp and find Spotted Calf, if he was still alive. If he was not, he would look for Yellow Horse. One way or another he had to convince them that he had not killed Running Buffalo. If he could do that, he would get a horse and head south. If he could not, then he wouldn't need the horse. He would be dead.

Duncan moved around the horses and approached the Comanche camp from the west. There were several fires burning low, and he could see only one guard, who was looking east, toward the burned-out station. Tommy moved closer to the camp, looking for Spotted Calf.

And then Tommy saw his adopted father propped up against the back rest that had been made for him. Duncan moved away into the long shadows cast by the fires among the brush and approached the older man from the rear. When he got very close, he removed his knife from its scabbard at the back of his neck and then crawled on his belly the final few feet to Spotted Calf.

Duncan grabbed Spotted Calf from behind, covering his mouth with his left hand and placing the flat side of the cold blade against the older man's throat.

"Do not make a sound," Duncan said softly in Comanche. "It is Swift Eagle, your son. I have come to find out why you hunt me and why so many brave warriors must die for nothing. I will not hurt you if you are quiet. I will take my hand from your mouth so that you can speak."

Duncan did just that, but he kept his knife at the warrior's throat. The older man turned his head to look at him.

"You can call yourself my son after you have killed Running Buffalo? Surely you do this to dishonor me," the older man said softly.

"I mean no dishonor to you or to Running Buffalo. I did not kill him."

"You lie like all white men," Spotted Calf said, his voice starting to rise.

"Keep your voice down," Tommy warned as he moved the knife a little to remind the older man that it was still there. "I do not lie to you. If I had killed Running Buffalo, would I have risked my life to come here tonight? Only a fool would do that, and I am not a liar or a fool."

Duncan wondered about the truth of at least half of his last statement. He probably was a fool, he thought.

"But Yellow Horse saw you riding away from Running Buffalo's body," Spotted Calf said. "You rode away and never returned, a sure sign that you killed my son."

Duncan thought for a moment, then said softly, "I will tell you how I came to leave your people. One day, Running Buffalo and I went out to hunt, just as we often did. We were not too far north of where we are now. We split up, again, as we often did. I saw nothing. After a while I called to him, but no one answered. I thought of searching for him, and then I thought of my parents and my sister who I had not seen in many years. I called out again. No one answered. I turned my pony north and rode away as fast as I could. I never turned back."

"Then why are you here now?" Spotted Calf asked. "Why have you come back into our lands?"

"I came back because I stole from the white men and they chased me here," Tommy answered. "Then Yellow Horse attacked me. If I had killed Running Buffalo, then I would have killed Yellow Horse, too. That I did not must prove to you that I am blameless."

"It is your word against that of my son, Yellow Horse," the older man said. "I cannot believe that Yellow Horse would lie, yet your words also sound true. How will I know what is true?"

Tommy knelt silently beside the warrior for two or three minutes, then spoke what was on his mind.

"We must leave it up to the spirit of Running Buffalo. Yellow Horse and I will have a trial by combat. If Yellow Horse wins, you will know that he spoke the truth and you will kill me. If I win, you will know that I spoke the truth and you will let me leave in peace. But however the fight ends, you will war no more against the white men of the station or against horse soldiers, who are sure to come. Is it agreed?"

Spotted Calf was silent for some time. He could not, would not, believe that Yellow Horse had lied, for if he had, then Yellow Horse would also be the one who had killed Running Buffalo, his brother. And yet Swift Eagle had made a good case for his innocence. If he had killed Running Buffalo, why had he not killed Yellow

Horse when he had the chance? Why had he come to this camp now instead of escaping once again? Surely these were good arguments in favor of Swift Eagle's case. Finally Spotted Calf spoke.

"It is agreed. You will stay here at my side until dawn. Then you and Yellow Horse will have a trial by combat just as you say."

Duncan took the knife from against the warrior's neck and returned it to its scabbard.

"You have decided wisely, my father," he said, "but my heart is heavy that you must watch as I fight my blood brother, Yellow Horse. I wish that there were some other way to show you the truth."

"There is no other way," Spotted Calf said. "I must send for Yellow Horse, so that he may prepare for the combat at dawn."

"Perhaps I should leave for a while, so that he will not do something foolish," Tommy suggested.

"Stay here and roll up in one of these blankets," Spotted Calf said. "He will not know who you are."

Duncan shrugged and did as he was told, trusting Spotted Calf would protect his life until dawn. As soon as he moved away from the older man and had covered up with a blanket, he heard the warrior call out for Yellow Horse. A brave not far from Duncan got up and went in search of him. He returned in a few minutes with Yellow Horse at his side.

"You sent for me, father?" the younger man asked respectfully.

"I did, my son," he answered. "Now sit here beside me while I tell you of the strange thing that just happened to me."

The young warrior did as he was bidden and his father told him all that had happened.

"And Swift Eagle is here, in this camp at this moment?" Yellow Horse exclaimed.

"He is very close to us, my son, and he will remain here safely until dawn, when we find the truth."

"But how could you doubt my word, father?" Yellow Horse asked.

"He could ask the same question of me, my son. The truth is that I no longer know who speaks true and who does not. I must trust that the spirit of Running Buffalo will show me who killed him. His hand will guide the knife of the one who speaks the truth. I pray that it may be you, Yellow Horse." The old man squeezed his son's arm.

"Where is the Swift Eagle?" Yellow Horse said loudly. "Is he afraid to show his face to me?"

Most of the camp was awake now, and Duncan sat up and threw the blanket away from him.

"I am here, Yellow Horse, and I am not afraid of you or your words. We will know that I speak the truth when the sun rises from the ground."

Yellow Horse leaped to his feet, pulled his knife, and sprang for Duncan.

But Duncan was on his feet, too. He had thought that Yellow Horse would not stand by while they waited for the dawn. He crouched as Yellow Horse lunged toward him.

The warrior leaped at Duncan, but he sidestepped and landed a glancing blow to Yellow Horse's left ear. The Indian sprawled in the dirt, then scrambled to his feet, crouching low with the knife glinting wickedly in his right hand.

"I will kill you now, white man," Yellow Horse snarled. "You are no longer my brother."

"I don't think you ever were," Tommy answered.

Then Yellow Horse attacked again. This time Tommy blocked the Indian's knife with his left forearm and threw a hard right fist straight from the shoulder that struck the Indian flush on the nose, breaking it and bringing tears to the man's eyes. Yellow Horse took a step backwards and Duncan stepped in, landing a left to the stomach and a hard right just below the warrior's heart.

Yellow Horse grunted in pain and stepped back again, but he held onto the knife. He knuckled the tears from his eyes with his left fist and then wiped at the blood that flowed freely from his shattered nose. Then he came at Duncan again.

This time the Indian feinted with the knife, then shifted it to his left hand and lunged. Duncan was ready for this, having watched Yellow Horse practice this maneuver for hours when they were boys. He blocked the knife with his right and landed a vicious left to the belly. The Indian dropped his guard and

Duncan hit him with another left to the belly and a hard right to the jaw. The Indian fell on his back in the dirt.

Duncan stepped back and waited as the Indian got slowly to his feet. He tottered there for a second, seemingly done in, then he threw a handful of dirt at Duncan's head and lunged again with the knife.

Duncan blocked most of the dirt with his left, but some got in his eyes. He forced himself not to blink as he stepped to his right just in time to avoid getting Yellow Horse's blade in the belly. As it was, the knife tore his shirt just above his belt.

Duncan danced away and wiped his streaming eyes. Yellow Horse followed, a look of determination on his face.

The Indian lunged again, and Duncan once more blocked the blow, then kneed the warrior viciously in the groin. The Indian dropped his knife and doubled up, a cry of pain escaping from his lips.

Tommy landed two solid uppercuts to the face, mashing the broken nose and breaking off teeth. Yellow Horse fell to the ground, dazed to the point where he could no longer resist. Duncan sat on the warrior's chest and pinned his arms to the ground with his knees. Then he drew his Arkansas Toothpick from the scabbard behind his neck and let the blade trace out the word "LIAR" lightly on the warrior's forehead. Blood seeped slowly into the cuts and then ran down the Indian's face.

Duncan rested the razor edge of the blade against the Indian's neck and said loudly to the warriors who gathered around them, "The spirit of Running Buffalo has guided me this night. It was he who helped me defeat his murderer. This man known to you as Yellow Horse killed his own brother, then blamed me for his treachery. It is he who is responsible for all the warriors who died or were wounded as you hunted me. It is he who has brought shame and death upon his tribe. And now Running Buffalo commands that I not kill his brother but give him to you. I do this out of respect for my brother, Running Buffalo."

Duncan got up and stepped away from Yellow Horse. The crowd of angry, muttering warriors parted as Spotted Calf limped into the circle and stopped by his son.

"Why, Yellow Horse, did you kill your own brother?" he asked, his voice choked and tears running down his cheeks.

Yellow Horse got to his feet and faced his father, swaying gently on his feet.

"Because he did everything right and I did nothing right," he answered. "Because you only saw him and never me. I hoped that with him gone you would see me and be my father, too."

"And for this you sacrificed your honor and the lives of many warriors in the tribe. It would have been better if you had never been born."

And then a knife gleamed dully in Spotted Calf's hand, and he plunged it into Yellow Horse's belly. He forced the blade up until it sliced into the young warrior's heart, stilling it forever.

"I gave you life and I take it away," the old man cried as Yellow Horse's lifeless form slid to the ground.

The camp was absolutely silent. Slowly, by ones and twos, the warriors drifted away, each deep in his own thoughts. Soon Duncan and Spotted Calf were left alone.

"You may go from here now, Swift Eagle," the old man said. "It is better that we never look upon each other again. The pain of the memory of this night would be too great. Take what horses you want and leave us now."

Duncan stood there, torn by the old man's sorrow.

"I'm sorry, Spotted Calf," he said. "I'm truly sorry."

The old man said nothing and did not even acknowledge that Duncan had spoken. Tommy walked slowly to the horse herd, found the saddle for Horton's and put it on the roan. When that was done, he found a couple of good horses for Harry and Pedro, too. He saw the grey that Horton had ridden at the beginning of the chase, and he took it for himself.

Angry Cougar came over to Duncan as he was leading the horses away from the herd.

"How did you get out of the trading post, Swift Eagle?" the warrior asked. "We watched for a long time, and no one came out. Your clothes and hair are not even singed. How is it possible that the flames never touched you?"

Duncan thought about that for a minute. Too much explanation might work against Pedro if there ever were any more problems with the Comanche.

"I think that the Great Spirit had other things for me to do besides to die in the flames," he finally answered. "He knew that I must clear my name. And Running Buffalo's spirit cried out for revenge. Because of that I was spared from the flames."

Angry Cougar thought about what he had just heard and decided that there was wisdom in the words. He also thought that Swift Eagle had been touched by the hand of the Great Spirit and should now be considered to be a great medicine man. Never had he heard of medicine as strong as that possessed by Swift Eagle. Angry Cougar told him just that.

"My medicine was strong for one purpose, my friend," Duncan said as he put his hand on the warrior's shoulder. "It might never be strong again. We must let the Great Spirit decide who he will use to do what he wants done. We cannot decide for him. Only time will tell if my medicine is strong forever."

The young brave nodded in agreement with the words of wisdom he had heard from the great medicine man. Duncan waved at the man, then he mounted his horse and rode away from the Comanche camp forever.

Chapter 21

Duncan had to travel less than a thousand yards in order to rejoin his companions, but in many ways, it was the longest journey he had ever made. In the course of those thousand yards, he left behind him forever the seven years he had spent living with the Comanches. He left behind an adopted father and the body of a brother gone bad, a brother who had killed his own brother in a fit of jealousy. That man, Running Buffalo, had been Duncan's constant companion and best friend.

Duncan also left behind him any chance of a normal life. Now he was headed back to the corral, back to the sheriff who would still expect to take him back to Benton, where he would get a swift trial and then quickly be hung with a new rope.

Duncan decided that he was not going back home to hang.

Tommy was not yet twenty, yet he had lived as a man for many years. Those had been tough years, first among the Comanche and then back among his own people, people who, in their suspicion of anything or anyone who had lived with the Comanche, could be more cruel than any Indian could ever be. Now it was time for him to experience life fully, to discover its joys and its sorrows. He wanted a wife and a family and something to show for his life besides a handbill with this picture and a reward on it. None of this could be his as long as he was a wanted man, and the only way he could stop being wanted was to die or to leave the country. Duncan preferred the latter.

Duncan came to the edge of the clearing and reined his horse to a stop. There was no sense in riding up to the corral before daylight. Someone might mistake him for a Comanche and shoot him down. He dismounted from his horse, tied all of the animals to the mesquite, rolled up in a blanket that he had taken with him from the Indian camp, and awaited dawn. It was then that the strain of the past week caught up to him. Gone was his need for vigilance. He was asleep in moments.

Horton had trouble keeping his eyes open. They burned fiercely, and he was so tired that he began to welcome the thought of death. The moon had long since set and the night was very black. Only the glow from the embers of the gutted station relieved the darkness.

The sheriff had a problem, and he tried to make his tired mind deal with it. At first, he thought that the Duncan kid had run off to pull his hair-brained scheme of drawing off the Comanches so that the rest of them could escape. But he had heard no shots. He had heard no great commotion from the Indian camp that would indicate that the kid had been captured and tortured. He was left with the thought that Duncan had run off to safety without a horse, leaving the rest of them there to do battle with the Comanches in the morning.

In a way Horton could not blame the kid. Duncan didn't have much in the way of options in front of him. If he stayed, he would die, and if he went back to Benton, he would hang. Only to the south lay safety. The lawman bet that the kid would be at Eagle Pass within forty-eight hours, maybe less if he had managed to get away with a horse or two.

Horton was almost glad. It would be a shame if the only survivors of this fight were Comanches. It had been a hard-fought battle between brave men. There was a kind of honor to be found there in the fight.

But there was no honor in the kid's flight. So, the dishonored would be the survivor. Somehow that didn't sound like justice to the lawman.

The sheriff eased a cartridge from one of the loops in his belt and tossed it at Pedro. He heard a grunt as it hit the sleeping man. A few seconds later, Pedro was beside him.

"You'd better take the watch, my friend," he said. "I'm all in."

"Go to sleep, then," Pedro replied. "Harry and I will keep watch. You will need all your strength for the morning. They will come with the dawn."

So, Horton, too, leaned back and fell into an exhausted sleep from which even a raging battle could not have drawn him.

Dawn came, and with it came some choices. Tommy Duncan got up and went over to his horses. He considered briefly swinging into the saddle and heading south, then put the idea aside. Come hell or high water, he was going to have to face Matt Horton, or he would never be able to stop looking over his shoulder. He tied his blanket behind his saddle and collected the reins of the horses. He began walking slowly towards the stone corral.

"Hello, the corral!" he yelled as he emerged into the clearing. "Hold your fire. It's me, Tommy Duncan." He kept walking directly toward the stone enclosure.

There was no sound from within, and Duncan was suddenly struck with the thought that perhaps Spotted Calf had gone back on his word to leave the white men alone. He knew better than that as soon as he'd thought of it. Spotted Calf was above all else a man of honor. Still, he wondered what he would find inside the corral.

Duncan walked to the mouth of the corral and looked inside. He was greeted by three smiling faces. Harry was the first to speak.

"I can't believe it's you, man! I thought you'd gone an' run off. An' here you are walkin' around as if there weren't a Indian within ten miles."

"I'd be surprised if they're even that close," Tommy answered. "The broke camp a couple of hours after I left here. I doubt that you could find 'em even if you tried."

"An' look at the horses!" Pedro added. "You got my roan back an' Matt's big grey an' a pair of horses that are even better than the ones that the Comanche stole. How'd you come by 'em?"

"To tell you the truth, Spotted Calf just gave 'em to me last night," Tommy answered.

"You're gonna try to tell me that you just walked into the camp, asked for horses, told 'em to leave, an' then they all went home?" Harry asked.

"It wasn't quite like that," Tommy said, and then he told them the whole story from the time he had left the corral the night before until he had gone to sleep at the edge of the clearing.

When he had finished, Duncan could tell that even Horton was impressed. Harry was absolutely overjoyed.

"Man, I knew for certain that I was a dead man last night. I wanted to go back home so bad I could taste it. In fact, if you'll give me one of them horses, I'll start out right now. How about it?"

"Sure," Tommy said. "You can have one of the mustangs. Sorry that I can't help you out with a saddle. Spotted Calf only had the one that was on Matt's horse."

"He can have mine," Horton said from the other side of the corral. "I'm not goin' to be able to use it for some time. Besides, Harry, you earned it. You've done a hell of a job in the last day or two, includin' savin' my bacon when Jack shot me. The saddle's the best I can do for you."

"An' you'll need some food an' money," Pedro added. He reached deep into his pocket and pulled out a handful of money.

"I took this back from Jack," he said. "It's yours. You earned every penny. I'd be dead if it wasn't for you."

"An' you wouldn't have a sore head if it wasn't for me, either," Harry said with some embarrassment. "I'm sorry for what I done, an' I don't deserve your money. You'd better keep it."

"Take it, Harry," Pedro insisted. "I want you to have it. If you ever get too much money, you can always send me some." The proprietor stuck the money in Harry's shirt pocket.

"Well, I'm thankin' all of ya," Harry said with some emotion. "An' I promise that I'll never go ridin' with the likes of Jack again. I'm done tryin' to be a badman."

Tommy and Pedro helped Harry saddle one of the mustangs and Horton filled the saddlebags with some of the food that Pedro had saved from the fire. When they were finished, Horton handed Harry the Winchester that he'd been using.

"You might need this on your way home. It'll be a good souvenir to remember this place by. Think about us from time to time an' come visit us in Benton if you're of a mind to. You'll always be welcome anywhere there's a Horton."

"Much obliged, sheriff," Harry said as he mounted. "But I expect I won't be back this way. This place scares me to death." He reined his horse through the gate and rode off due east. He never looked back.

"That boy grew up pretty good yesterday," Horton observed.

"He's a good man, sure enough," Pedro added, and Tommy nodded in agreement.

"We'd better get ready to leave when the stage gets here," Horton said. "Thanks to Pedro we got new clothes. Let's set about usin' em."

The men changed clothes and Tommy retrieved his guns from where he had left them the night before. Pedro changed the bandage on Horton's wounds. There was no sign of infection, but the proprietor produced a bottle of Irish whiskey and, after taking a healthy pull at it himself, poured a little on the wounds. Horton nearly passed out from the pain, but he knew that the whiskey would help fight infection.

"It's a whole lot smoother on the inside," Pedro said, as he handed the bottle to the sheriff, "so maybe you should try that, too."

Horton took a pull and coughed.

"Didn't notice a whole lot of difference," he grimaced.

"Some folks got no taste an' no manners," Pedro said as he took back the bottle and put it away. "We'll save the rest for the stage ride."

"You'll be makin' that ride without me," Tommy announced in a firm voice. "I'll be riding' south just as soon as I can put some food in a sack and get aboard one of these horses."

"You're forgettin' somethin', ain't you, boy?" Horton said. "You're my prisoner, an' you're supposed to be goin' back with me so's you can stand trial."

"I'm not goin' back there to hang, Matt," the kid said. "I've told you that all along. You'd all be dead but for my talk with Spotted Calf last night. The least you owe me is a runnin' start for the border."

"An' you should remember that we wouldn't of been in this fix in the first place if you hadn't tried to rob the bank," Horton reminded him. "What I owe you is justice, nuthin' more."

"An' just what is justice, Matt?" Tommy asked. "An' just where am I supposed to find it? It sure ain't at the end of a rope. I'm goin' to leave now. I've got my guns, but I'll keep my word to you, Matt. I won't use them to escape. But if you're gonna stop me from leavin', you'll have to kill me. Make up your mind, 'cause in one minute I'm ridin' out."

Horton eased his Colt from its holster and thumbed back the hammer. "You're not leavin' like that," he said evenly.

"Goodbye, Matt," Tommy said as he started to turn away.

Horton fired only once.

It was two o'clock before the weekly stage arrived in a cloud of billowing dust. Jose Garcia, the driver, pulled the six-horse rig to a stop in front of the charred shell of the station. Pete Lonigan, riding shotgun, jumped to the ground and went up to the lead team. They were due for a change of teams at Cedar Station, but it was quite plain that there would be no fresh horses to be found in the barn today.

The driver got down from the box and walked over to Pedro, who was patting smooth the dirt mounded over a fresh grave. There was another just like it alongside.

"What in the hell happened here?" the driver wanted to know.

"We had some Comanche troubles here yesterday, but I reckon that they're all over now. The Indians left last night an' won't be back, I'm told."

"Who's in there," the driver asked as he pointed to the fresh graves.

"That one there," Pedro said as he pointed to the other grave, "has got the only Comanche body they left behind. He died in the corral yonder. This one here's got one of ours in it. The sheriff over there's just finishin' up the marker."

Matt Horton walked over to the men slowly, carrying the board awkwardly. Pedro took it from the lawman and put an end into a shallow hole at the head of the grave, then shoveled dirt in around it. He stomped the dirt down good and then stepped back. The words carved crudely into the plank read, "Thomas Duncan. Died 1873. A good man in a fight."

"Who was this Duncan fellow?" the driver wanted to know.

"Just a man who was in the wrong place at the wrong time," Horton said tersely. "Let's get out of here."

The driver looked around as Pedro threw the few possessions he had left into the stage and helped Horton aboard. He walked over to Pedro as he was starting to climb in after the lawman.

"You goin' to rebuild, Pedro?" he asked. "This is sure a good spot for a relay post."

Pedro O'Brien stepped back down and looked around the place for a last time, then shook his head slowly.

"There's no way, Jose," he answered. "As far as I'm concerned, I'm done with this place for good. You're drivin' the last stage from Cedar Station."

"Can't say that I blame you none," the driver said. "There ain't much in the way of help close by when trouble comes."

Jose Garcia and Pete Lonigan climbed onto the box while Pedro stepped up into the stage. Jose cracked his whip and the horses began to pull the stage slowly away from Cedar Station. Nothing moved behind them. All that remained were the dead.

Chapter 22

It took more than a week for that last stage from Cedar Station to finally get to Benton. Pedro O'Brien had left the stage in Austin to catch up with his wife and hired man. He had decided that he would move to San Antonio and run a cantina there. Horton suspected that he'd do well, as long as his wife was close by to make sure that he didn't drink up the profits.

As for Horton, the trip had been a hard one. The constant bouncing had been hard on his wounds, but by the time they had reached Austin, Pedro had been able to remove the stitches that had closed the knife wound across his chest, and the bullet wound was little more than a nuisance. He was still very weak, however, and he was glad that he had not been riding a horse all the way back from Cedar Station.

The stage had a two-day layover in Austin, and as soon as he arrived Horton got a bath and a change of clothes, then visited a doctor who pronounced sagely that he was in real danger of living. After that he spent the rest of the time in a room at the Driscoll Hotel, sleeping in a real bed with clean sheets. By the time the stage pulled out again for Benton, the sheriff thought that he was close to living up to the doctor's pronouncement.

It was late afternoon when the stage pulled up in front of the depot in Benton. Horton climbed down from his perch on the box where he had been riding with the driver and then waved goodbye. He turned then and walked slowly up the street to his office. His deputy, Carl Butcher, was lounging in a chair near the door. When he saw Horton, he bounded to his feet and walked over to him.

"Glad you're back, Matt!" he said enthusiastically as he reached for the lawman's Henry. "I'll clean this an' put it away for you."

"Just put it away, Butch," Horton said. "It's clean enough as it is. Then go get Mayor Pflugg for me, will you?"

"Sure thing, Sheriff," the deputy said eagerly. Then, almost as an afterthought, he asked, "Did you ever catch up with Tommy Duncan?"

Horton stepped into his office and sat down carefully in his chair. It felt good to sit in something that wasn't moving.

"Yeah," he said finally, "I found him."

The deputy looked puzzled, then said, "Then where is he?"

"Just go get Mayor Pflugg like I told you, damn it!" he exploded, and was instantly sorry to have taken his bad temper out on his deputy. It was too late to apologize, however, for the deputy was already out of the door and headed down the street towards the mayor's office.

Carl Butcher was back with the mayor in tow in less than ten minutes. Horton made an apology to his deputy for hollering and then told the men to take a seat. When they were comfortable, the sheriff began telling them the story of what had happened during the chase. It took more than an hour, for he left nothing out as far as he knew. He stopped the story with the final showdown at the corral.

"So, you were wounded and the kid wouldn't come back with you, is that it, Matt?" the mayor asked.

"That's about the size of it," he answered. "I wasn't in no shape to fight him or even to argue, so I drew down on him an' he started to mount up an' ride away."

"So, you killed him tryin' to escape?" the deputy said.

"There's a grave out front of that burned-out station with his name on it," Horton said in agreement. "I did what I had to do. I didn't like it, but I did it anyway."

"I'm sure that you did the only honorable thing you could do under the circumstances," the mayor said soothingly. "And I'm sure the whole town will feel the same way, although I'm afraid that Claire will take this whole thing pretty hard. She set a lot of store by that boy Tommy."

"He wasn't no 'boy,' Rufus," Horton said testily. "He saved my bacon an' O'Brien's, too. He was a hell of a man in my book, an' he deserved better than to die in the dust in the middle of nowhere."

"It was his choice, none the less," Pflugg said with determination. "He could have come back with you to stand trial. The jury certainly would have taken his actions into account."

"Do you really think so?" Horton asked skeptically.

The mayor thought for a minute, then said, "I guess not. Nothing would change the fact that the teller was dead and that Tommy Duncan was part of the gang that did it. They'd have hung him, too, right alongside the other fellow, if you'd gotten back a couple of days earlier."

"Glad I missed it," Horton said. "I never could stomach a hangin'." He said no more, but sat in his chair, deep in thought.

Pflugg and Butcher sat in uneasy silence for a while, then got up and walked out of the office. Horton stayed on, trying to come up with just the right thing to say to Claire. He'd been working on that speech for more than a week, and he still didn't know what he was going to say. Finally, he gave up and pushed himself out of his chair. He walked slowly through the doorway and out onto the street. He decided that there was no sense facing Claire on an empty stomach, so he headed for Marta's Cafe for dinner.

He ate his meal in silence, interrupted only by townspeople who came by to pat him on the back and welcome him home. It seemed that the story of what had happened had been spread all over town in a matter of half an hour. Not for the first time Horton was impressed by the people's propensity for gossip.

He finally finished what was on his plate, paid the protesting Marta for the meal, and began walking toward Claire's house. He still did not know what he was going to say. He climbed the stairs to her porch and knocked at the door.

Claire was suddenly there in front of him, more lovely than ever. Horton felt an ache for her and wanted to take her in his arms, but he could not do anything but just stand there like some big, dumb ox.

Claire was crying. "You have some nerve coming here," she said angrily, "after what you've done."

"I don't know what someone's told you, Claire," Horton said, "but I'd like to tell you what really happened."

"Don't bother," she replied. "Mayor Pflugg has told me the entire story, including how Tommy was a hero and saved everybody in the station. And then you rewarded him by murdering him! They should get a rope and hang you, Matt Horton. But you're already dead. You've got no heart! Now go away and never speak to me again. If you ever set foot on my property, I'll shoot you down like the dog you are!" And with that she slammed the door in his face.

Horton stood there for a moment longer, then turned on his heel and walked slowly back to the office. As he went, he relived the final sequence of events that had taken place in the corral.

When Horton fired that final shot, he fired it into the air. Tommy stopped dead in his tracks, then turned in resignation to face Horton.

"You're not goin' back to Benton, Tommy, but you ain't goin' to Mexico, either," the sheriff said. "You're gonna take my gray an' ride out west, to California maybe, or better yet, to the Oregon Territory. When you get there, send me a wire. Call yourself a Horton an' let me know where you are. I'll send you some cash an' a letter of credit. You can find a place to raise good horses for us out there. If you want, later on you can buy me out. If not, then you can just manage the place for me."

Tommy was astounded. "But how're you gonna explain this back in Benton?"

"There's a body in those ashes," Horton said as he pointed to the shell of the station. "We'll bury him under a board with your name on it. It'll be probably the only decent thing Jack has ever done."

"But Claire—what about her?" Tommy said with real concern.

"I'll tell her what really happened. You send her a letter after you get set up in Oregon. Just remember, from now on you're a Horton, not a Duncan. You lost your name when you tried to be a badman."

"It's a small price to pay, I guess," Tommy said. "Besides, I'm gettin' a good one to replace it. I don't know how to thank you, Matt."

"Just don't hold up no more banks," the sheriff said as he put his Colt away. "I can't stand this much excitement very often."

Pedro had walked over and shaken the kid's hand.

"Tell you what, Tommy," Pedro said. "Help me bury Jack an' I'll give you the roan, too. That way you'll get to Oregon a lot faster. We'll fix you up with some food an' money, too, so you'll not be tempted to stop on the way. An' you can pick up your saddle back down the trail."

And so, Jack had taken Duncan's place in the grave, and it was Tommy Horton who had ridden off to Oregon and a new life.

Horton walked into his office and sat there in the growing darkness, thinking about Claire. In a few months she'd be getting a letter from Tommy and then she'd feel pretty foolish. Maybe then she'd come to apologize for what she had said. Or perhaps by then she would have found someone else to comfort her. Right then Horton was too tired to care one way or the other.

The sheriff got up and lit a pair of lamps, then went over to the gun rack and took down his old 10-gauge shotgun. He broke it open to check the loads, then snapped it closed.

It was time to make the early rounds. Horton had to make them, regardless of how he felt. It was what an honorable man was expected to do.

~ The End ~

About the Author

Colonel R.C. Hartjen joined the Army at age 17 and was commissioned six years later. He has commanded an Armored Cavalry troop in Germany, an Airborne Cavalry troop in Viet Nam, and a tank battalion in the United States.

He holds an earned doctorate in counseling psychology and is a graduate of the US Army War College. *The Last Stage From Cedar Station* is the second novel in his Horton Family historical western series, and follows *Cowhouse Creek Showdown*.

Colonel Hartjen is retired and makes his home in Leavenworth, Kansas along with his wife, Helen, and their devoted yellow labrador, Annie.